PENGUIN CLASSICS

DAISY MILLER

HENRY JAMES was born in 1843 in Washington Place, New York, of Scottish and Irish ancestry. His father was a prominent theologian and philosopher, and his elder brother, William, is also famous as a philosopher. He attended schools in New York and later in London, Paris and Geneva, entering the Law School at Harvard in 1862. In 1865 he began to contribute reviews and short stories to American journals. In 1875, after two prior visits to Europe, he settled for a year in Paris, where he met Flaubert, Turgenev and other literary figures. However, the next year he moved to London, where he became so popular in Society that in the winter of 1878–9 he confessed to accepting 107 invitations. In 1898 he left London and went to live at Lamb House, Rye, Sussex. Henry James became a naturalized citizen in 1915, was awarded the Order of Merit, and died in 1916.

In addition to many short stories, plays, books of criticism, autobiography and travel, he wrote some twenty novels, the first published being *Roderick Hudson* (1875). They include *The Europeans, Washington Square, The Portrait of a Lady, The Bostonians, The Princess Casamassima, The Tragic Muse, The Spoils of Poynton, The Awkward Age, The Wings of the Dove, The Ambassadors* and *The Golden Bowl*.

GEOFFREY MOORE was born in London. After war service in the RAF he read English at Cambridge. His career as an academic included appointments at the universities of Wisconsin, Tulane, New Mexico, Southern California, Kansas and Harvard. In 1955 he became the first full-time lecturer in American literature at a British university (Manchester), and from 1962 to 1982 he was Professor of American Literature at the University of Hull. He also ran a weekly arts programme on American radio, and edited and produced for BBC Television. He was a contributor to *The Times Literary Supplement* for many years. His publications include *Poetry from Cambridge in Wartime* (1947), *The Penguin Book of Modern American Verse* (1954), *Poetry Today* (1958), *American Literature and the American Imagination* (1964), *American Literature* (1964) and *The Penguin Book of American Verse* (1977; revised, 1983). Geoffrey Moore was General Editor for the works of

Henry James in Penguin and, in addition to *Daisy Miller*, edited and introduced *Roderick Hudson* and *The Portrait of a Lady* for Penguin Classics.
Geoffrey Moore died in 1999.

PATRICIA CRICK, one-time Scholar of Girton College, Cambridge, is a
teacher of modern languages.

HENRY JAMES

Daisy Miller

Edited with an Introduction by
Geoffrey Moore
and Notes by Patricia Crick

Penguin Books

PENGUIN BOOKS

Published by the Penguin Group
Penguin Books Ltd, 80 Strand, London WC2R 0RL, England
Penguin Putnam Inc., 375 Hudson Street, New York, New York 10014, USA
Penguin Books Australia Ltd, 250 Camberwell Road, Camberwell, Victoria 3124, Australia
Penguin Books Canada Ltd, 10 Alcorn Avenue, Toronto, Ontario, Canada M4V 3B2
Penguin Books India (P) Ltd, 11 Community Centre, Panchsheel Park, New Delhi – 110 017, India
Penguin Books (NZ) Ltd, Cnr Rosedale and Airborne Roads, Albany, Auckland, New Zealand
Penguin Books (South Africa) (Pty) Ltd, 24 Sturdee Avenue, Rosebank 2196, South Africa

Penguin Books Ltd, Registered Offices: 80 Strand, London WC2R 0RL, England

www.penguin.com

First published 1878
Published in Penguin Books 1974
Reprinted in Penguin Classics 1986
33

Introduction copyright © Geoffrey Moore, 1986
Notes copyright © Patricia Crick, 1986
All rights reserved

Printed in England by Clays Ltd, St Ives plc
Filmset in VIP Palatino

CONTENTS

INTRODUCTION

In the latter part of 1878, when *Daisy Miller* had been pirated in both New York and Boston, William Dean Howells wrote to his friend James Russell Lowell:

There has been a vast discussion in which nobody felt very deeply, and everybody talked very loudly. The thing went so far that society almost divided itself into Daisy Millerites and anti-Daisy Millerites. I was glad of it for I hoped that in making James so thoroughly known, it would call attention to the beautiful work he had been doing so long for very few readers.

Howells is referring to the fact that, although James had been publishing since 1864, when he was twenty-one years old, his career had so far lacked the *cachet* which success with a wide public can sometimes bring.

Daisy Miller supplied that lack. Of all James's fictions it was the most immediately popular. I say 'fictions', although the term is slightly ponderous, because it is neither a novel nor a short story but half-way between – what most critics today call a 'novella' and James, in his Preface to the New York edition, a 'nouvelle'. Short though it is, I am convinced that it must stand on its own for it is a little masterpiece, sounding what Rebecca West, in her book on the novelist published in 1916, called 'the pure note of the early James, like a pipe played carefully by a boy'.

James had published several books before *Daisy*, apart from reviews and critical pieces: *A Passionate Pilgrim, and*

Other Tales and *Transatlantic Sketches* in 1875; *Roderick Hudson* and *The American* in 1876; and *Watch and Ward* (a reprint of the 1871 magazine publication) in 1878. All were written in the manner which is the keynote of the early James and which Richard Poirier called his 'comic sense' – that is, the style is down-to-earth, ironical, bordering on the Dickensian, but the characters are rather obviously symbolic of attitudes or states of mind: Roderick Hudson of the genius of the artist, Christopher Newman of the spirit of the New World, and so on. Daisy Miller, by contrast – although she might, like Isobel Archer, be argued to be representative of the innocence and lack of sophistication of America confronted by the corruption of Europe – is, on the surface at least, brilliantly lifelike.

It was, as he tells us, in Rome in the summer of 1877 that James conceived the idea of Daisy. He heard from his friend Alice Bartlett a piece of gossip about an American 'child of nature and of freedom' who had picked up a 'good-looking Roman, of vague identity'. A pencil note by his jotting down of this 'donnée' enjoined him to 'Dramatize, dramatize!' – and this he did, in London, in the winter of 1877–8. He sent off the story to *Lippincott's* magazine in Philadelphia assuming, apparently, that since he had had so much success with his submissions to William Dean Howells for the *Atlantic Monthly*, all doors in America were open to him. Not so *Lippincott's*, however, the editor of which sent it back to him with a rejection slip. Sensitive as no other to the nuances of his time, James must have had an inkling of the reason ('an affront to American womanhood') for, instead of promptly sending it on to Howells, he gave it to his London friend Leslie Stephen, who published it in the magazine of which he was the editor: *The Cornhill Magazine* (June–July 1878).

This had its advantages and disadvantages. It made

James the literary lion of London but it lost him a great deal of money. As soon as the book was received in the United States it was published without any payment there being no copyright laws in existence at the time. Leon Edel notes that when Harper's brought it out in their 'Half Hour Series' it sold 20,000 copies 'in a matter of weeks'. After that, as Edel goes on to say, 'Henry James was to be considered by the world "a sufficiently great man".' He is quoting from a letter which Henry wrote to his brother William in January 1878. Ironically, he almost certainly did not have *Daisy Miller* but rather *Roderick Hudson* in mind when he wrote those words for, as he was later to say, being praised for *Daisy* was like being praised for one's rhinestones while the real treasures of one's jewel-case were being ignored. Still, this little thing that he tossed off and consistently underrated did in a most surprising way hit the mark. As *The Great Gatsby* is to *Tender is the Night* so *Daisy Miller* is to *The Portrait of a Lady*.

It begins equally casually but, understandably – given the fifty or so years difference in time – more in the manner of Washington Irving than of Fitzgerald's idol, Ring Lardner. 'As many travellers will remember' is, indeed, very much the style of Irving at the beginning of *The Legend of Sleepy Hollow*. It is particularly appropriate that the scene should be set in Vevey, for Vevey is a sort of no man's land, half-way between the grim certainties of Geneva and the moral laxity of Rome. If we have not realized at the beginning that the author is an American, we become aware of it by the end of the fourth sentence. Vevey assumes in June 'some of the characteristics of an American watering-place'; it evokes an echo of Newport or Saratoga. But there is a difference. Among the stylish young girls in their muslin flounces there are Russian princesses; and the Dent du Midi and the Château de

Chillon rise majestically above the Hotel Trois Couronnes, as it stands by the waters of Lake Geneva.

It is in the garden of this hotel that we are introduced to the 'hero', Winterbourne. Although in the New York edition James added the Christian names of 'Frederick Forsyth' he is never anything but 'Winterbourne' in the original version. And this is entirely appropriate for he is an archetypal figure borne on the wind of winter from icy Geneva into this magic world of Vevey. He is twenty-seven years old and has come to see his aunt; apparently he is of independent means for he has been 'studying' in Geneva for some years. He has been to both school and college there so, like James himself, he is not a very typical American. At the moment that we meet him he is enjoying an after-dinner coffee and a cigarette. A small, pale boy of about nine years old walks into his line of vision. Although he is wearing knickerbockers, the boy is nothing like Little Lord Fauntleroy; he carries an alpenstock which he thrusts into everything he comes near. Seeing Winterbourne, he stops by his table and asks him for a lump of sugar. His voice is sharp, hard and immature yet 'somehow not young'; from his accent Winterbourne deduces him to be American. After some trivial conversation on the subject of sugar and teeth the boy announces that his sister is approaching. Winterbourne is struck by her appearance and thinks, not 'How pretty she is!' but 'How pretty they are!' – an early indication of his attitude.

This beautiful vision that has swum across Winterbourne's horizon chides her brother for kicking up gravel as he vaults over his alpenstock, and Winterbourne, formal to the last, considers himself 'in a manner presented'. The girl, however, continues to address herself to her brother, asking him whether he means to take 'that pole' to Italy. ' "Are you going to Italy?" ' asks Winterbourne, 'in a tone of great respect', and, further, ' "Are

you – a – going over the Simplon?" ' This means little to
Daisy, for she takes the Simplon to be a mountain. James
allows Winterbourne to dwell at length on the young girl
whom fate has thrown in his way. What is strange to him
is the fact that her eyes can be 'singularly honest and
fresh' and her glance 'perfectly direct and unshrinking',
yet she herself be manifestly not immodest. Is it possible,
he thinks, that she is a coquette? But no – there is no hint
of mockery in her 'bright, sweet, superficial little visage'.
She presents a problem – and a challenge – to Winterbourne. He tries to learn more by asking her brother his
name and finds that it is Randolph C. Miller. His sister
is Annie P. Miller, more often called Daisy, and their
father is a rich businessman in Schenectady, New York.
They have been travelling around for some time 'in the
cars'. As Daisy speaks, Winterbourne cannot take his
eyes off her. His besotted state, however, does not
obscure the sharpness of his observation. When Daisy
says that she feels as if she were in Europe whenever she
puts on a Paris dress Winterbourne replies rather archly
that it is as if it were 'a kind of wishing-cap'. The words
which follow (' "Yes," said Miss Miller, without examining this analogy') exactly hit off Daisy's nature and at the
same time provide a good example of the irony which
pervades this deceptively simple tale.

It is at this point, one-eighth of the way through the
story, that the reader begins to perceive what James is
about. He has already given us a clue through the general
nature of Winterbourne's comment on the Daisy-type;
he has set the story in neutral territory between two
opposing ways of life, the Genevan and the Roman; he
has even given us a miniature Garden of Eden in the
grounds of the Trois Couronnes. As for Winterbourne
himself, he has lived in Europe so long that he has
become 'dishabituated to the American tone'. At one
moment he is inclined to take Daisy at face-value and

at another to see her as 'a designing, an audacious, an unscrupulous young person'.

Meanwhile Daisy, always herself, and unaware of the acute moral dilemmas she causes in the minds of highly respectable young gentlemen, asks Winterbourne whether he has been to 'the old castle'. She means, of course, the Château de Chillon across the lake, about whose prisoner, Bonnivard, Byron wrote so movingly. Winterbourne offers to take her, noting that she does not bridle, 'blushing as a young girl at Geneva would have done'. But – eternal problem – how to dispose of the little brother? Perhaps he could stay with Eugenio, the Millers' courier? At this point the courier comes on the scene to announce that luncheon is served. When Daisy says that she is going to Chillon with Winterbourne, the courier's manner is offensive. But Daisy is not to be put down:

'Oh well, we'll go some day,' said Miss Miller. And she gave him a smile and turned away. She put up her parasol and walked back to the inn beside Eugenio. Winterbourne stood looking after her; and as she moved away, drawing her muslin furbelows over the gravel, said to himself that she had the *tournure* of a princess.

Having promised Daisy that he will introduce her to his aunt (a singular honour!) Winterbourne dutifully makes the attempt. It is typical of Winterbourne that he should wish to do so. Anyone less naïve would have known in advance what her reaction would be. Her very name, Costello, connotes the upper echelons of the New York 400; her appearance is classic ('a long, pale face, a high nose, and a great deal of very striking white hair'). She has certainly seen the Millers – and their courier – she informs her nephew, and has kept out of their way!

Winterbourne is more respectful and attentive to his aunt than is her own son – not, one hopes, out of any immediately crass motive but for what is perhaps an even less pressing one: 'he had imbibed at Geneva the idea that one must always be attentive to one's aunt'. This counterpointing of the formality and primness of Winterbourne with the noble savagery of Daisy (a sort of female Natty Bumppo) is all the more effective for being set in the *tableau vivant* atmosphere of Vevey. The very fact that Mrs Costello ('a person of much distinction who frequently intimated that, if she were not so dreadfully liable to sick headaches, she would probably have left a deeper impression upon her time') holds her nephew in such high esteem tells us a lot about him.

Her venom towards Daisy is shocking because it is directed against a sitting target. It does not matter that she is very pretty; Mrs Costello considers her 'common', and that's an end to it. She is, in fact, so common that Mrs Costello cannot understand where 'they' get their taste – another indication of how Daisy, this little flower of the field, is being made into a type. Mrs Costello is not too old, she gives her nephew to understand, to be shocked. By what, pray? Well, first, by the fact that the Millers treat their courier like one of the family when, as everyone knows, he should be treated as the English treat their servants – either with patronizing condescension or as if he were not there. Second, by the fact that Daisy has talked to Winterbourne without an introduction and, third, that she has agreed to go to Chillon with him after only half an hour's acquaintance. 'What a dreadful girl!' exclaims Mrs Costello. All Winterbourne can stammer in reply is that she is 'wonderfully pretty' and 'completely uncultivated' – as, indeed, she is. Although Daisy comes from urban Schenectady, she might as well be Annie Oakley for all Mrs Costello understands of her. However, Winterbourne's fascination overcomes his fear of disapproval. Looking for Daisy, he finds her

in the garden, wandering about in the warm starlight, like an
indolent sylph, and swinging the largest fan he had ever
beheld.

This sybaritic and implicitly erotic description says it
all. Winterbourne is smitten, although he is far too fearful
to do anything about it. To make matters worse, Daisy is
extremely keen to meet Mrs Costello, and chatters on
about her:

Winterbourne was embarrassed. 'She would be most happy
but I am afraid those headaches will interfere.'

In the end, Daisy gets the message:

Her prettiness was still visible in the darkness; she was opening and closing her enormous fan. 'She doesn't want to know
me!' she said suddenly. 'Why don't you say so? You needn't
be afraid. I'm not afraid!' And she gave a little laugh.
Winterbourne fancied there was a tremor in her voice . . .

He is shocked and mortified, refusing to meet her
honesty with honesty, and maintaining to the end that
Mrs Costello's health is the reason. Although Daisy takes
it very well, she is upset by this deliberate insult. It is our
first indication of how ruthless her fellow Americans can
be and how in the end they will triumph and, through
their antagonism, perhaps contribute materially to her
death. Her courtesy contrasting with Mrs Costello's
rudeness, Daisy introduces Winterbourne to her mother
and as she does so he notes that for all her so-called
'commonness' she has a 'singularly delicate grace'. The
mother is

a small, spare, light person with a wandering eye, a very exiguous nose, and a large forehead, decorated with a certain
amount of thin, much frizzled hair.

It is this kind of description which makes the first edition
of *Daisy* such a delight. The prose is down-to-earth,

unadorned – in contrast to the New York edition of the novel where, in attempting to supply *nuances* which he felt he had missed in his first version, James succeeded more often than not in gilding the lily. Two examples from the pages just covered will illustrate the point:

1878 edition

' . . . She's gone somewhere after Randolph; she wants to try to get him to go to bed. He doesn't like to go to bed.'

'Let us hope she will persuade him,' observed Winterbourne.

New York edition [1909]

'She's gone somewhere after Randolph; she wants to try to get him to go to bed. He doesn't like to go to bed.'

The soft impartiality of her constatations, as Winterbourne would have termed them, was a thing by itself – exquisite little fatalist as they seemed to make her. 'Let's hope she'll persuade him,' he encouragingly said.

1878 edition

The young girl looked at him through the dusk. 'But I suppose she doesn't have a headache every day,' she said, sympathetically.

Winterbourne was silent for a moment. 'She tells me she does,' he answered at last – not knowing what to say.

Miss Daisy Miller stopped and stood and looked at him. Her prettiness was still visible in the darkness; she was opening and closing her enormous fan. 'She doesn't want to know me!' she said suddenly. 'Why don't you say so? You needn't be afraid. I'm not afraid!' And she gave a little laugh.

Winterbourne fancied there was a tremor in her voice; he was touched, shocked, mortified by it. 'My dear young lady,' he protested, 'she knows no one. It's her wretched health.'

The young girl walked on a few steps, laughing still . . .

New York edition [1909]

The girl looked at him through the fine dusk. 'Well, I suppose she doesn't have a headache every day.'

He had to make the best of it. 'She tells me she wonderfully does.' He didn't know what else to say.

Miss Miller stopped and stood looking at him. Her prettiness was still visible in the darkness; she kept flapping to and fro her enormous fan. 'She doesn't want to know me!' she then lightly broke out. 'Why don't you say so? You needn't be afraid. I'*m* not afraid.' And she quite crowed for the fun of it.

Winterbourne, however, distinguished a wee false note in this; he was touched, shocked, mortified by it. 'My dear young lady, she knows no one. She goes through life immured. It's her wretched health.'

The young girl walked on a few steps in the glee of the thing . . .

First thoughts are best. It is always a chastening experience to compare a writer's first and last versions. Theoretically, the skill and experience of the older man ought to be preferable; but it is almost never the case, and James's attempts to supplant the fine clarity of James I with the cloying additives of the Old Pretender are a persistent irritant to the reader who tries his hand at detailed analysis and comparison. It is all the more remarkable since James is always telling us to 'Present, present!'; 'talking about', he insists, is not enough. But he did not always practise what he preached.

Daisy announces to her mother that she is going to the Castle of Chillon with Winterbourne and he offers to take the mother too. She refuses and Winterbourne thinks how different her attitude is from that of

the vigilant matrons who massed themselves in the forefront of social intercourse in the dark old city at the other end of the lake.

To Winterbourne's amazement Daisy clamours to be 'taken out in a boat' there and then:

Her face wore a charming smile, her pretty eyes were gleaming, she was swinging her great fan about . . .

She is sexually – albeit innocently – aroused and this is
communicated to Winterbourne.

'Do, then, let me give you a row,' he said to the young girl.
'It's quite lovely, the way you say that!' cried Daisy.
'It will be still more lovely to do it.'
'Yes, it would be lovely!' said Daisy.

Their mood is shattered by the voice of the courier,
who effectively puts a stop to the expedition, underlining
what the American colony considers the disgraceful way
in which the Millers allow the hired help to run their
lives. But what they cannot see, and what James so
clearly brings out, is that there is a complete lack of
awareness in the Millers that they are doing anything
wrong. As they leave under Eugenio's wing, Winterbourne puzzles over Daisy's 'sudden familiarities and
caprices'. He feels that he would 'enjoy deucedly' going
off with her somewhere.

Two days later he does take her on the projected trip
to Chillon. She has unfortunately asked him to meet her
in the hall of the hotel where the couriers, the servants
and the foreign tourists are lounging about and staring.
As Daisy trips down the stairs, 'buttoning her long
gloves, squeezing her folded parasol against her pretty
figure', Winterbourne feels 'as if there were something
romantic going forward. He could have believed he was
going to elope with her.' No such luck. He is far too much
of a Caspar Milquetoast to trust his instincts. He allows
Geneva and his sainted aunt to reach out their long arms
again, while Daisy, little girl that she is, chatters away,
persuading Winterbourne to take her on the steamer
rather than in a carriage.

Winterbourne, almost against his nature, takes
extreme delight in Daisy's company while at the same

time noticing that, although she is 'extremely animated', she is not – as she had seemed on the occasion of suggesting the night trip – thoroughly excited. Winterbourne, in other words, is looking for some evidence that will damn Daisy for being a loose woman and yet at the same time wishing with all his heart for a romantic entanglement. Again, no such luck. Daisy might be a flirt but she is not a coquette, nor does she disgrace him with her commonness; she simply sits there looking beautiful and delivering herself 'of a great number of original reflections'. She chides Winterbourne for being so solemn and receives the reply that he was never better pleased in his life. Winterbourne really means it, and Daisy is delighted.

At Chillon she shows herself to be all female,

[flirting] back with a pretty little cry and a shudder from the edge of the *oubliettes* and [turning] a singularly well-shaped ear to everything that Winterbourne told her about the place.

She listens to Winterbourne's travelogue about Bonnivard and Chillon but the questions that she asks are about his family, 'his previous history, his tastes, his habits, his intentions'. She is no less forthcoming about herself; she even wonders whether he will travel round with them, and possibly teach Randolph.

At these advances Winterbourne goes back in his shell, telling her that he has engagements which will force him to go back to Geneva the very next day. Daisy is greatly piqued by this information. She thinks him horrid – and not without reason, for his conduct and demeanour have led her to believe that he is interested in her. There can be no other reason for his sudden departure than the presence of another woman in Geneva! Daisy has, of course, unwittingly hit the mark and Winterbourne is bewildered by her perspicacity and also by her 'extraordinary mixture of innocence and crudity'. Finally, she tells him that she will stop 'teasing' him if he will promise to come to Rome in the winter. Winterbourne, whose plans already include visiting his aunt in Rome at that time, has no difficulty in agreeing.

When he arrives towards the end of January, his aunt has already been established there for several weeks. Daisy, she informs him, 'goes about alone with her foreigners' and when she is invited to a party 'she brings with her a gentleman with a good deal of manner and a wonderful moustache'. To his aunt's proclamation that the Millers are 'very dreadful people', Winterbourne replies:

'They are very ignorant – very innocent only. Depend upon it they are not bad.'

Mrs Costello cares only that they are vulgar; 'whether or no being hopelessly vulgar is being "bad" is a question for the metaphysicians'.

Winterbourne is cast down by his aunt's news that Daisy is surrounded by 'half a dozen wonderful moustaches'. In his imagination she had been anxiously awaiting his arrival. He goes to call on other friends first, at the house of one of whom 'in a little crimson drawing room, on a third floor' the Millers are announced. During the subsequent conversation Daisy chides Winterbourne for being mean, and he remembers an axiom that American women 'are at once the most exacting in the world and the least endowed with a sense of indebtedness'. He was mean, he learns, because he would not stay in Vevey. Winterbourne is put out. Has he come all the way to Rome to encounter her reproaches? Daisy announces that she is coming to a party to be given by Mrs Walker and wishes to bring 'an intimate friend' of hers – a Mr Giovanelli, 'the handsomest man in the world – except Mr Winterbourne!' In fact, she is off to meet him in the Pincio that very afternoon. Mrs Walker and her mother both advise her against it. It is the hour when all Rome is on the streets – the late afternoon – and there is danger of the Roman fever, too. Daisy offers to compromise by allowing Winterbourne to come with her to the meeting.

Winterbourne strolls through the curious Roman crowd with Daisy on his arm, enjoying the occasion very much indeed, sure in his own mind that he is not going to hand her over to Giovanelli. To her light banter ('Why haven't you been to see me? You can't get out of that'), he is as stiff as a board ('I have had the honour of telling you that I have only just stepped out of the train'). Daisy rightly points out that he has had time to call on Mrs Walker first. Winterbourne begins to explain that he knew Mrs Walker in Geneva – as if that were relevant to the game of love and flirtation. But Daisy cuts him short; she knows all that. Good-tempered child that she is, she simply prattles (James's verb) about the splendour of their rooms at the hotel and how they are going to stay all winter if (second warning reference) they do not all die of the Roman fever. James, who in his later magisterial phase lost interest in differentiating between one person's conversation and another's, is here at his best in representing Daisy's flow of delightful, albeit inconsequential, small talk. If we have not fallen in love with her by this time it is not James's fault. Her allusions are all in character. As Chillon was 'that castle' so the guides in Rome are 'dreadful old men that explain about the pictures and things'. As they pass the gate of the Pincian Gardens she says to Winterbourne, 'We had better go to that place in front where you look at the view.'

They see Giovanelli in the distance. He is

a little man standing with folded arms, nursing his cane. He had a handsome face, an artfully poised hat, a glass in one eye, and a nosegay in his button-hole.

When Winterbourne announces his intention of staying with Daisy she is not in the least troubled. She does,

however, say that he is being 'too imperious'. With unusual seriousness she tells him that she has never allowed
a gentleman to dictate to her or to interfere with anything
she does. Giovanelli advances with 'obsequious rapidity'
and Winterbourne tells her that he is not the right one
for her.

The odd threesome stroll along together, each observing the other. Giovanelli keeps his temper down and the
conversation up; he is the soul of courtesy and politeness. Nevertheless Winterbourne's reaction (as might be
expected) is not favourable. Initially it might as well be
Mrs Costello speaking:

He is not a gentleman . . . he is only a clever imitation of
one. He is a music-master, or a penny-a-liner, or a third-rate
artist.

but the coda is pure combatant male: 'Damn his good
looks!' What chiefly puts Winterbourne out is the fact
that Daisy cannot distinguish between a real gentleman
and an imitation one; it does not enter his head that she
might not care. Her standards are of the heart and not of
the head, and Giovanelli, despite his designs on American heiresses (into which category he might presume
Daisy to fall), is not a bad man. Winterbourne worries
away at the fact that, by the formal standards of both
Geneva and Rome, a nice girl ought to know the difference and if she doesn't – or, worse, if she doesn't care –
then she probably isn't a nice girl, and what is Winterbourne doing knowing her anyway? A nice girl would
not make a rendezvous with a 'presumably low-lived
foreigner'. It was impossible to regard Daisy as a perfectly well-conducted young lady; she was wanting in a
certain 'indispensable delicacy'. But we knew that
already – at least from the Geneva-Costello-Walker point
of view. If she would only try to get rid of him in order
to be with her 'lover' he would have his answer. But her

conduct confounds him. She continues to enjoy herself with the two men in a spirit of 'childish gaiety' until a carriage draws up beside them and a flushed Mrs Walker beckons Winterbourne over.

Her agitation ('It is really too dreadful . . . That girl must not do this sort of thing. She must not walk here with you two men. Fifty people have noticed her') antagonizes Winterbourne. He thinks, despite his own previous reservations, that Mrs Walker is making too much of a fuss. When she dramatically announces that Daisy is ruining herself Winterbourne insists on Daisy's fundamental innocence. Mrs Walker ignores this and maintains that she is crazy – and her mother too. She has come in a last-minute attempt to save Daisy. This of course is fine dramatic stuff, for Daisy, the delightful Daisy, is doomed. Poe said that the death of a beautiful woman was the most affecting subject for literary art, and it looks as if James has stumbled on the formula.

Daisy is summoned to the carriage, and Giovanelli goes with her. Mrs Walker tries to inveigle Daisy into accompanying her. Daisy, however, announces that it is enchanting to stay as she is. There follows a superbly simple piece of writing in which James exactly renders the feeling of the occasion:

'It may be enchanting, dear child, but it is not the custom here,' urged Mrs Walker, leaning forward in her victoria with her hands devoutly clasped.

'Well, it ought to be, then!' said Daisy. 'If I didn't walk I should expire.'

'You should walk with your mother, dear,' cried the lady from Geneva [note the attribution, although Mrs Walker is in fact American], losing patience.

'With my mother dear!' exclaimed the young girl. Winterbourne saw that she scented interference. 'My mother never walked ten steps in her life. And then, you know,' she added with a laugh, 'I am more than five years old.'

'You are old enough to be more reasonable. You are old enough, dear Miss Miller, to be talked about.'

Daisy looked at Mrs Walker, smiling intensely. 'Talked about? What do you mean!'

That 'smiling intensely' hits it off exactly. It is the first crack in Daisy's armour; the first time it has been borne into her that she really is doing something which, in the eyes of the Western world of the 1870s, is immoral. The previous insult from Mrs Costello she had seen in a purely personal light and not as an indictment of her whole way of life. From that moment on, two-thirds of the way through the *novella*, she is in decline. Giovanelli bows 'to and fro, rubbing his gloves and laughing very agreeably' but Winterbourne thinks it 'a most unpleasant scene' – as indeed it is, and a crucial one – the scene of the tying of the Aristotelian knot. It is to get more unpleasant yet. Daisy decides that, like Bartleby the Scrivener, she would prefer not to know what Mrs Walker means. Here is the authentic voice of the James heroine. Mrs Walker blunders on:

'Should you prefer being thought a very reckless girl?' she demanded.

'Gracious me!' exclaimed Daisy. She looked again at Mr Giovanelli: then she turned to Winterbourne. There was a little pink flush in her cheek; she was tremendously pretty. 'Does Mr Winterbourne think,' she asked slowly, smiling, throwing back her head and glancing at him from head to foot, 'that – to save my reputation – I ought to get into the carriage?'

This, as I have indicated, is an important moment in the drama, the scene around which all else turns; not only the lifting of the scales from Daisy's eyes, but a testing of her moral fibre. When Winterbourne tries to tip the balance by advising her to get into the carriage, Daisy says with dignity:

'I never heard anything so stiff! If this is improper, Mrs Walker,' she pursued, 'then I am all improper, and you must give me up.'

Good for Daisy! Like Huckleberry Finn who took a stand against his society by helping Jim to escape and thus spoke out against slavery, Daisy strikes a blow for the ultimately-to-be-liberated female, who may· flout the rules as much as she wishes, because her intentions are honest. But there is a danger in the flouting of convention, as Shelley discovered fifty years before.

Winterbourne is summoned into the protective confines of Mrs Walker's carriage. 'That was not clever of you,' he says candidly when he is inside. But Mrs Walker is unperturbed. Daisy has gone too far. For a month she had been

. . . flirting with any man she could pick up; sitting in corners with mysterious Italians; dancing all the evening with the same partners; receiving visits at eleven o'clock at night . . .

Winterbourne takes Daisy's part; her only fault is that she is very uncultivated. Mrs Walker sees Daisy as 'naturally indelicate'; she should not have made it a personal matter that Winterbourne had forsaken her in Vevey. 'I suspect, Mrs Walker,' says Winterbourne, 'that you and I have lived too long at Geneva!'

Mrs Walker wants Winterbourne to stop seeing Daisy but he refuses to do so because he likes her 'extremely'. She then lets him out of the carriage, as it reaches 'that part of the Pincian Garden which overhangs the wall of Rome and overlooks the beautiful Villa Borghese'. Daisy and Giovanelli are there. Winterbourne watches them as they stand at the parapet in apparent intimacy, Giovanelli holding Daisy's parasol over both their heads and letting it rest on her shoulder. When he begins to walk, however, it is not towards them but towards the residence of his aunt. He has made his choice.

Three days later Mrs Walker's party takes place and despite the *contretemps* in the carriage Winterbourne puts in an appearance. Mrs Miller, her hair 'more frizzled than ever', comes alone ('Daisy just pushed me off by myself'). 'And does not your daughter intend to favour us with her society?' asks Mrs Walker, acting the *grande dame*. Daisy and Giovanelli, says Mrs Miller, are at home, she at the piano, he singing: ' "I guess they'll come before very long," concluded Mrs Miller hopefully.'

Mrs Walker announces that when Daisy does come she will not speak to her, but when the girl arrives, after eleven o'clock, she has no option, for Daisy 'rustles forward in radiant loveliness, smiling and chattering, carrying a large bouquet and attended by Mr Giovanelli'. Everyone stops talking and turns to see what will happen. Daisy talks to Mrs Walker as if nothing had happened, telling her how she and Giovanelli have been practising and ending with 'Is there anyone I know?' 'I think everyone knows you!' says Mrs Walker acidly. Giovanelli sings uninvited; Daisy talks through his performance. She wants to dance, but Winterbourne says he can't. No, says Daisy, it's because he is too 'stiff'. They talk about the incident of three days before. When Winterbourne says that Giovanelli would never have asked 'a young lady of this country to walk about the streets with him', Daisy comes into her own:

'About the streets?' cried Daisy with her pretty stare. 'Where then would he have proposed to her to walk? The Pincio is not the streets, either; and I, thank goodness, am not a young lady of this country. The young ladies of this country have a dreadfully poky time of it, so far as I can learn; I don't see why I should change my habits for *them*.'

'I am afraid your habits are those of a flirt,' said Winterbourne gravely.

'Of course they are,' she cried, giving him her little smiling stare again. 'I'm a fearful, frightful flirt! Did you ever hear of a

nice girl that was not? But I suppose you will tell me now that
I am not a nice girl.'

'You're a very nice girl, but I wish you would flirt with me,
and me only,' said Winterbourne.

'Ah! thank you, thank you very much; you are the last man
I should think of flirting with. As I have had the pleasure of
informing you, you are too stiff.'

'You say that too often,' said Winterbourne.

He goes on to tell her that flirting is 'a purely American
custom; it doesn't exist here'. Daisy retorts that she and
Giovanelli are not flirting. They are – and she has used
the phrase before – 'very intimate friends':

'Ah,' rejoined Winterbourne, 'if you are in love with each
other it is another affair.'
She had allowed him up to this point to talk so frankly that
he had no expectation of shocking her by this ejaculation; but
she immediately got up, blushing visibly, and leaving him to
exclaim mentally that little American flirts were the queerest
creatures in the world . . .

He has touched Daisy on a sore spot. She and Giovanelli are not 'lovers'. She has never given a thought to
the down-to-earth sexuality implied by such a relationship. She calls his mention of such a possibility 'disagreeable'. Winterbourne is bewildered by this turn of events
and stands staring until Daisy is rescued by Giovanelli,
who offers her tea. They sit together 'in the embrasure
of the window, for the rest of the evening', ignoring the
rest of the company. When it comes to the time for everyone to go Mrs Walker turns her back on Daisy. Oblivi-
ous of, or wishing to override, the calculated insult, Mrs
Miller thanks her hostess profusely. But Daisy, as
Winterbourne sees, is

. . . too much shocked and puzzled even for indignation. He
on his side was greatly touched.

After this Winterbourne goes often to the Millers'

splendid rooms at the hotel. Giovanelli is always there, alone with Daisy – yet she is never embarrassed or annoyed by his coming upon them in this way. She seems to be as happy with the two of them as with the one. Winterbourne, who has never met a girl like this before, thinks that she would probably not be a jealous person. The women he had met before Daisy had made him afraid; he felt that he would never be afraid of Daisy, and this leads him to the appalling conclusion that she would prove in the end to be 'a very light young person'.

On Sunday afternoon, at St Peter's with his aunt, Winterbourne notices Daisy and Giovanelli. Mrs Costello, after inspecting them through her eyeglass, says cuttingly:

'He is very handsome. One easily sees how it is. She thinks him the most elegant man in the world, the finest gentleman. She has never seen anything like him; he is better even than the courier. It was the courier probably who introduced him, and if he succeeds in marrying the young lady, the courier will come in for a magnificent commission.'

Winterbourne is sure that Daisy has not thought of marrying Giovanelli, and that he in his turn does not hope to marry her. This remark provokes Mrs Costello into a remarkable piece of insight and a typically cynical conclusion:

'You may be very sure she thinks of nothing. She goes on from day to day, from hour to hour, as they did in the Golden Age. I can imagine nothing more vulgar . . .'

Winterbourne is equally (but in his case untypically) perspicacious in his reply:

'If she thinks him the finest gentleman in the world, he, on his side, has never found himself in personal contact with such splendour, such opulence, such expensiveness as this young lady's. And then she must seem to him wonderfully pretty and interesting. I rather doubt whether he dreams of marrying her. That must appear to him too impossible a piece of luck. He has nothing but his handsome face to offer, and there is a substantial Mr Miller in the mysterious land of dollars. Giovanelli knows that he hasn't a title to offer. If he were only a count or a *marchese*! He must wonder at his luck at the way they have taken him up.'

At this singular moment of truth Winterbourne is able to observe, despite his infatuation, that

' . . . Daisy and her mamma have not yet risen to that stage of – what shall I call it? – of culture, at which the idea of catching a count or a *marchese* begins. I believe that they are intellectually incapable of that conception.'

Later, he is sickened to hear the innuendoes about Daisy as Mrs Costello sits on a 'little portable stool at the base of one of the great pilasters' and a dozen of the American colony in Rome come to talk with her. It is painful to him 'to hear so much that was pretty and undefended and natural assigned to a vulgar place among the categories of disorder'. When he hears that Daisy has been sitting with Giovanelli 'in the secluded nook in which the great papal portrait (of Innocent X by Velazquez) is enshrined' he rushes round to the Millers, but of course Daisy is out. Mrs Miller utters the fateful word which Winterbourne's aunt has used earlier. (Mrs Costello had said, 'Depend on it that she may tell you any moment that she is "engaged"'; Mrs Miller says, 'I keep telling Daisy she's engaged.') Winterbourne wants to know what Daisy's views on this are and receives the reply that Daisy says she *isn't* engaged. But 'she goes on as if she was' says Mrs Miller, who regards Giovanelli as a 'real gentleman'. She has made him promise to tell her if they really are engaged because 'I should want to write to Mr Miller about it – shouldn't you?' Winterbourne's reply is a masterpiece of Jamesian 'put down':

> . . . he certainly should; and the state of mind of Daisy's mamma struck him as so unprecedented in the annals of parental vigilance that he gave up as strictly irrelevant the attempt to place her upon her guard.

Exactly so. And in the sum total of human experience it is odd that Winterbourne should ever have taken any interest in such a common girl, given the fact that he and his aunt are such proper American 'aristocrats'. For an English aristocrat, of course – as the social history of the upper classes in the late nineteenth century shows – the fact that Daisy is a child of the *nouveau riche* would probably not have mattered.

After this, Winterbourne does not see Daisy for some time, their 'common acquaintances' having decided to ostracize her in an endeavour to prove to 'observant Europeans' that her outrageous conduct is not representative of Americans. In the remainder of the same paragraph, James expresses with all the elegance and insight of which he is capable Winterbourne's bewilderment in the face of her being 'carried away' by Giovanelli:

> He said to himself that she was too light and childish, too uncultivated and unreasoning, too provincial, to have reflected upon her ostracism or even to have perceived it. Then at other moments he believed that she carried about in her elegant and irresponsible little organism a defiant, passionate, perfectly observant consciousness of the impression she produced. He asked himself whether Daisy's defiance came from the consciousness of innocence or from her being, essentially, a young person of the reckless class. It must be admitted that holding oneself to a belief in Daisy's 'innocence' came to seem to Winterbourne more and more a matter of fine-spun gallantry. As I have already had occasion to relate, he was angry at finding himself reduced to chopping logic about this young lady; he was vexed at his want of instinctive certitude as to how far her

eccentricities were generic, national, and how far they were
personal . . .

By now it is springtime in Rome and Winterbourne has
been there since late January. Strolling in the Palace of
the Caesars he encounters Daisy with (of course) Giovanelli. She chides him for always going about alone.
Giovanelli conducts himself, as always, with the utmost
courtesy, carrying himself 'in no degree like a jealous
wooer'. In fact, he strolls away to pick a sprig of almond
blossom in order to allow Winterbourne to speak to Daisy
alone.

Daisy does not believe that her compatriots are really
shocked. They are only pretending; they do not really
care what she does. Winterbourne maintains that they
do, and that they will show it – disagreeably. When Daisy
wishes to know what he means by this he asks her
whether she has not noticed anything. 'I have noticed
you,' replies Daisy. 'But I noticed you were as stiff as an
umbrella the first time I saw you.' The unconscious sex-
ual reference, conflating as it does the more customary
'stiff as a poker' cliché with the evocation of damp Cal-
vinistic Geneva, and coming after all the other references
to stiffness, reminds us how very much affected by Daisy
Winterbourne is, despite all his prissy reservations. He
warns Daisy that her compatriots will give her the cold
shoulder if she does not mend her ways. For some
reason, this seems to affect Daisy more than we should
have thought, given her habitual flouting of convention.
She begins to colour, recalling the incident at Mrs
Walker's party, and wishes that Winterbourne would say
something to prevent it. He has already, he says, telling
them that Mrs Miller believes that Daisy and Giovanelli
are engaged. Daisy agrees that this is what Mrs Miller
thinks and Winterbourne asks, laughing, whether Randolph believes it, too. Daisy replies that Randolph does

not believe anything but since Winterbourne has mentioned it, she *is* engaged to Giovanelli. This immediately stops Winterbourne's laughter:

> 'You don't believe it!' she added.
> He was silent a moment; and then, 'Yes, I believe it!' he said.
> 'Oh, no, you don't,' she answered. 'Well, then – I am not!'

What *is* one to do with such a contrary girl? She leaves, with Giovanelli. A week later Winterbourne is returning from dinner at a villa on the Caelian Hill. It is eleven o'clock and such a beautiful night that he decides to walk via the Colosseum. As he stands there enjoying the atmosphere of the arena he remembers that it is unwise to linger too long because of the 'villainous miasma'. Then, on the steps of the cross in the centre of the Colosseum, he notices two figures. They are, of course, Daisy and Giovanelli. They comment on the way that Winterbourne is looking at them, without realizing who it is. He stops

with a sort of horror; and, it must be added, with a sort of relief . . . She was a young lady whom a gentleman need no longer be at pains to respect. He stood there looking at her – looking at her companion, and not reflecting that though he saw them vaguely, he himself must have been more brightly visible. He felt angry with himself that he had bothered so much about the right way of regarding Miss Daisy Miller. Then, as he was going to advance again, he checked himself; not from the fear that he was doing her injustice, but from a sense of the danger of appearing unbecomingly exhilarated by this sudden revulsion from cautious criticism.

Daisy recognizes him and exclaims that he has cut them. Immediately, he assumes that Daisy is putting on an air of injured innocence – 'clever little reprobate' that she is. However, he decides to try to save her from the malaria and remonstrates with Giovanelli for allowing her to stay out in the pernicious Roman air. 'I told the

Signorina it was a grave indiscretion;' Giovanelli replies, 'but when was the Signorina ever prudent?' Daisy declares that she was never sick and doesn't mean to be. She just had to see the Colosseum by moonlight, and she has had 'the most beautiful time'. She appeals to Giovanelli, significantly still calling him 'Mr' and thus giving the lie to Winterbourne's constantly recurring suspicions. If there is any danger, Eugenio the courier can give Daisy some pills. Poor trusting Daisy! If there ever was an illustration of the axiom: 'Take what you want,' said God, 'and pay for it later', it is the case of Daisy Miller. Winterbourne advises her to drive home as fast as possible. There follows a curious passage which seems to indicate that but for Winterbourne's timidity and obtuseness Daisy need not have been 'carried away' by Giovanelli. In the midst of her chatter about the beauty of the Colosseum she suddenly interjects, '*Did* you believe I was engaged the other day?' Winterbourne, who has begun to laugh at her attaching so much import-ance to seeing the ruin by moonlight, says that it doesn't matter what he believed the other day. What does he believe now, Daisy wants to know. Cruelly, Winter-bourne replies:

'I believe that it makes very little difference whether you are engaged or not!

At this point Giovanelli hurries forward, pressing her to get back to the hotel before midnight; if they do, they will be 'quite safe'. As she leaves, Daisy says 'in a strange little tone', ' "I don't care whether I have Roman fever or not!" '

It is her epitaph. A day or two later Winterbourne learns that 'the little American flirt' is dangerously ill. He goes to the hotel where Mrs Miller, surprisingly calm and composed, tells him that Daisy has been speaking of him. She wants Winterbourne to know

' . . . that she never was engaged to that handsome Italian. I am sure I am very glad; Mr Giovanelli hasn't been near us since she was taken ill. I thought he was so much of a gentleman; but I don't call that very polite! A lady told me he was afraid I was angry with him for taking Daisy round at night. Well, so I am; but I suppose he knows I'm a lady. I would scorn to scold him. Anyway, she says she's not engaged. I don't know why she wanted you to know; but she said to me three times – "Mind you tell Mr Winterbourne." And then she told me to ask if you remembered the time you went to that castle, in Switzerland. But I said I wouldn't give any such messages as that. Only, if she is not engaged, I'm sure I'm glad to know it.'

A week later Daisy is dead and Winterbourne goes to her funeral. Giovanelli is there, looking very pale. The passage which follows provides us with the truth about Daisy and at the same time gives the lie to Winterbourne's 'certainty' as to her immorality. Giovanelli says:

'She was the most beautiful young lady I ever saw, and the most amiable.' And then he added in a moment, 'And she was the most innocent.'
Winterbourne looked at him, and presently repeated his words, 'And the most innocent?'
'The most innocent!'

If Daisy had lived Giovanelli would have got nothing, he says:

'She would never have married me, I am sure.'
'She would never have married you?'
'For a moment I hoped so. But no, I am sure.'

As he speaks Winterbourne stares at what James calls 'the raw protuberance among the April daisies' – a disturbing, almost obscene contrast between the newly dug, teeming earth of the grave and the dead virginity of the girl who lies underneath.

Winterbourne leaves Rome and the following summer meets his aunt again at Vevey. They speak of Daisy. It has been on his conscience that he had done her an injustice:

> 'She sent me a message before her death which I didn't understand at the time. But I have understood it since. She would have appreciated one's esteem.'
> 'Is that a modest way,' asked Mrs Costello, 'of saying that she would have reciprocated one's affection?'
> Winterbourne made no answer to this question; but he presently said, 'You were right in that remark you made last summer. I was booked to make a mistake. I have lived too long in foreign parts.'

Despite this last statement – and it is not the first time that James has mentioned Winterbourne's alienation from his native land – he goes back to live in Geneva. It is said that 'he is "studying" hard – an intimation that he is much interested in a very clever foreign lady'. He has, in other words, given in to the grim forces of Geneva, the weight of convention; he has turned his back finally on openness and honesty.

For us, the readers, it is Daisy who is on the side of the angels, and I am sure that James meant it to be so, despite the fact that he invoked poetic justice in consigning her to her doom for being such a wicked flouter of convention and, later, in his 1907 preface, waved the whole thing aside as being 'pure poetry' anyway. What Americans at the time objected to, and why *Lippincott's* magazine rejected the story, was the fact that James had made Daisy so attractive whereas the *type* that she represented was anything but. Leon Edel makes much of what he describes as 'the total abdication, by the mass of American parents, of authority over their children'. But this is to miss the point; this is to see Daisy, once again, as a type. She is much more than this, as James so clearly shows – and it comes out best of all in the defiant little speech which Daisy makes to Mrs Walker on the Pincio: 'If this is improper, Mrs Walker, then I am all improper, and you must give me up.'

It has been noted more than once that James tends to identify himself with his heroines – and this is certainly true of Daisy. Ignorant and uncultivated as she is, she nevertheless has the courage to be herself – which is more than one can say of Winterbourne. At her level James imbues Daisy with something of his own spirit, which he expressed so well in his letter to the students of the Deerfield Summer School eleven years after the *novella* made such a dramatic impact on the Anglo-American public:

Oh, do something from your point of view; an ounce of example is worth a ton of generalities; do something with the great art and the great form; do something with life. Any point of view is interesting that is a direct impression of life. You each have an impression coloured by your individual conditions; make that into a picture, a picture framed by your own personal wisdom, your glimpse of the American world. The field is vast for freedom, for study, for observation, for satire, for truth . . . I have only two little words for the matter remotely approaching to rule or doctrine; one is life and the other freedom . . .

There is an echo here of Emerson: 'We will walk on our own feet; we will work with our own hands; we will speak our own minds.' If there is one abiding theme which runs through the American experience it is that men and women must have the courage to go it alone, setting their faces resolutely against what they see as arbitrary and outmoded rules and regulations. Daisy Miller is a slight piece, perhaps, to place such a burden of meaning on – a little flat, and certainly untouched by the tensions of James's more ambitious works. Yet it is all the more effective in conveying a message because of the very plainness and lucidity of its style.

At the end of Chapter I, James describes Daisy as a

princess. It is apt. She marks the first appearance in literature of the American Princess, the Heiress of all the
Ages. True, she does not have the intelligence of Isobel
Archer, nor the *panache* of the Princess Casamassima, but
she has spirit, and she has a charm which transcends her
ignorance. Mrs Costello will have it that she is as common as her name, but Mrs Costello is a dried-up harridan
'liable to sick headaches'. How old is Daisy Miller? – as
one might say, 'How many children had Lady Macbeth?'
Perhaps if she had been mature the epithet 'common'
might have had a modicum of relevance but I cannot see
her as being older than her late teens; her spontaneity
still has its first innocence. It is in his decision to treat her
not as one of her own 'type' but as a special case that
James shows his genius. *Daisy Miller*, ultimately, is a
story about America, about a way of life which made
its children, and especially the girl-children, as different
from Europeans as chalk from cheese.

Despite his consistent bachelorhood and the warmth
of his letters to young men, James was fascinated by
women – and they were fascinated by him. In the seven
weeks that he spent in Italy before he returned to London
to write *Daisy Miller* he rode often in the Campagna (car-
peted, incidentally, with daisies). He was reviving happy
memories of the early seventies in the same spot – from
which he wrote to his loving family in Quincy Street,
Boston: 'I am now in the position of a creature with *five*
women *offering* to ride with me.' Many women wrote him
letters and he was consulted about his views on them; it
is small wonder, then, that the American reading public
divided itself into 'Daisy Millerites' and 'anti-Daisy Millerites' in the autumn of 1878.

After *The American* and *Roderick Hudson* – in which the
women play second fiddle to the dashing heroes – *The
Europeans*, *An International Episode* and *Daisy Miller* high-
light the heroines. Gertrude and the Baroness in *The*

Europeans, Bessie Alden in *An International Episode,* and Daisy herself, are characters in the round. Mary Garland of *Roderick Hudson* is a positive Griselda and Christina Light is under the thumb (ultimately) of her mother. But Daisy is as independent and individual as her name is common or garden. Isobel Archer and Henrietta Stackpole in *The Portrait of a Lady* carry the delineation of female character a stage further. *Daisy Miller,* then, is the first of a series of studies of the American female which extend through the Princess Casamassima to Milly Theale in *The Wings of the Dove.* Leslie Fiedler, in *Love and Death in the American Novel,* claimed that American novelists lacked the ability to portray women realistically. He was thinking of them in the context of their relationship to men. Ironically – apart from his friend Howells – it is the suspected homosexual, James, who comes nearest to filling the gap to which Fiedler rightly points.

In *Daisy Miller* there is the seed of what we are to find in full bloom at the end of his career – not only in *The Wings of the Dove,* but also in *The Golden Bowl*: the pitting of the values of America against those of Europe. The reason Daisy has nothing in common with her fellow Americans in Rome is because they subscribe to the European way of looking at life, a way which so many of James's novels reveal to be shallow, superficial and cynical. Daisy is honest, fresh and open; like a female Sir Galahad her strength is as the strength of ten because her heart is pure. Let us allow Fiedler to have the last word since he, of all the American critics, is most concerned with the mythical and archetypal patterns of American fiction:

Daisy is . . . the prototype of all those young American female tourists who continue to baffle their continental lovers with an innocence not at all impeached, though they have taken to sleeping with their Giovanellis as well as standing with them in the moonlight. What the European male fails to understand is that the American Girl is innocent by definition, *mythically* innocent; and that her purity depends upon nothing she says or does . . .

GEOFFREY MOORE

NOTE ON THE TEXT

Immediately he had finished writing *Daisy Miller* in the spring of 1878, Henry James sent it to *Lippincott's* magazine in Philadelphia. Upon its being rejected, he gave it to his friend Leslie Stephen who published it in the magazine of which he was the editor, *The Cornhill Magazine* (XXXVII, June 1878, pp. 678–98 and XXXVIII, July 1878, pp. 46–7). Shortly afterwards in the same year the story was pirated by *Littell's Living Age* in Boston and the *Home Journal* in New York. Later in 1878 it was published in book form by Harper's in the United States and, in 1879, by Macmillan's in England. Between then and the early 1900s, when James minutely revised the story for the New York edition, *Daisy Miller* was reprinted many times – even appearing as a play (privately in England in 1882 and in the *Atlantic Monthly* in 1883). The dramatic version was as much of a flop as the fictional one was a success.

Having made a comparison of the New York edition (vol. XVIII, 1909) with the earlier version, I have decided (see Introduction, pp. 14–16) to reprint *Daisy* in its original form. Although James conscientiously attempted to supply for the definitive edition the psychological depth and nuances which he felt were lacking in the 1878 version, he succeeded only in burying the unassuming simplicity of his early style under the mannerisms of the Master. Not only – in my estimation – is the 1878 version superior as a work of art; it is also truer to James's original conception of Daisy's character.

G.M.

PREFACE TO
THE NEW YORK EDITION

It was in Rome during the autumn of 1877; a friend then
living there but settled now in a South less weighted with
appeals and memories happened to mention – which
she might perfectly not have done – some simple and
uninformed American lady of the previous winter,
whose young daughter, a child of nature and of freedom,
accompanying her from hotel to hotel, had 'picked up'
by the wayside, with the best conscience in the world, a
good-looking Roman, of vague identity, astonished at
his luck, yet (so far as might be, by the pair) all innocently, all serenely exhibited and introduced: this at least
till the occurrence of some small social check, some inter-
rupting incident, of no great gravity or dignity, and
which I forget. I had never heard, save on this showing,
of the amiable but not otherwise eminent ladies, who
weren't in fact named, I think, and whose case had
merely served to point a familiar moral; and it must have
been just their want of salience that left a margin for the
small pencil-mark inveterately signifying, in such con-
nections, 'Dramatize, dramatize!' The result of my recog-
nizing a few months later the sense of my pencil-mark
was the short chronicle of *Daisy Miller*, which I indited
in London the following spring and then addressed, with
no conditions attached, as I remember, to the editor of a
magazine that had its seat of publication at Philadelphia
and had lately appeared to appreciate my contributions.

That gentleman however (an historian of some repute) promptly returned me my missive, and with an absence of comment that struck me at the time as rather grim – as, given the circumstances, requiring indeed some explanation: till a friend to whom I appealed for light, giving him the thing to read, declared it could only have passed with the Philadelphian critic for 'an outrage on American girlhood'. This was verily a light, and of bewildering intensity; though I was presently to read into the matter a further helpful inference. To the fault of being outrageous this little composition added that of being essentially and pre-eminently a *nouvelle*; a signal example in fact of that type, foredoomed at the best, in more cases than not, to editorial disfavour. If accordingly I was afterwards to be cradled, almost blissfully, in the conception that *Daisy* at least, among my productions, might approach 'success', such success for example, on her eventual appearance, as the state of being promptly pirated in Boston – a sweet tribute I hadn't yet received and was never again to know – the irony of things yet claimed its rights, I couldn't but long continue to feel, in the circumstance that quite a special reprobation had waited on the first appearance in the world of the ultimately most prosperous child of my invention. So doubly discredited, at all events, this bantling[1] met indulgence, with no great delay, in the eyes of my admirable friend the late Leslie Stephen[2] and was published in two numbers of the *Cornhill Magazine* (1878).

It qualified itself in that publication and afterwards as 'a Study'; for reasons which I confess I fail to recapture unless they may have taken account simply of a certain flatness in my poor little heroine's literal denomination. Flatness indeed, one must have felt, was the very sum of her story; so that perhaps after all the attached epithet was meant but as a deprecation, addressed to the reader, of any great critical hope of stirring scenes. It provided

for mere concentration, and on an object scant and superficially vulgar – from which, however, a sufficiently
brooding tenderness might eventually extract a shy
incongruous charm. I suppress at all events here the
appended qualification – in view of the simple truth,
which ought from the first to have been apparent to me,
that my little exhibition is made to no degree whatever
in critical but, quite inordinately and extravagantly, in
poetical terms. It comes back to me that I was at a certain
hour long afterwards to have reflected, in this connec-
tion, on the characteristic free play of the whirligig of
time. It was in Italy again – in Venice and in the prized
society of an interesting friend, now dead, with whom I
happened to wait, on the Grand Canal, at the animated
water-steps of one of the hotels. The considerable little
terrace there was so disposed as to make a salient stage
for certain demonstrations on the part of two young girls,
children *they*, if ever, of nature and of freedom, whose
use of those resources, in the general public eye, and
under our own as we sat in the gondola, drew from the
lips of a second companion, sociably afloat with us, the
remark that there before us, with no sign absent, were a
couple of attesting Daisy Millers. Then it was that, in my
charming hostess's prompt protest, the whirligig, as I
have called it, at once betrayed itself. 'How can you liken
those creatures to a figure of which the only fault is touch-
ingly to have transmuted so sorry a type and to have, by
a poetic artifice, not only led our judgement of it astray,
but made *any* judgement quite impossible?' With which
this gentle lady and admirable critic turned on the author
himself. 'You *know* you quite falsified, by the turn you
gave it, the thing you had begun with having in mind,
the thing you had had, to satiety, the chance of "observing": your pretty perversion of it, or your unprincipled
mystification of our sense of it, does it really too much
honour – in spite of which, none the less, as anything

charming or touching always to that extent justifies itself, we after a fashion forgive and understand you. But why *waste* your romance? There are cases, too many, in which you've done it again; in which, provoked by a spirit of observation at first no doubt sufficiently sincere, and with the measured and felt truth fairly twitching your sleeve, you have yielded to your incurable prejudice in favour of grace – to whatever it is in you that makes so inordinately for form and prettiness and pathos; not to say sometimes for misplaced drolling. Is it that you've after all too much imagination? Those awful young women capering at the hotel-door, *they* are the real little Daisy Millers that were; whereas yours in the tale is such a one, more's the pity, as – for pitch of the ingenuous, for quality of the artless – couldn't possibly have been at all.' My answer to all which bristled of course with more professions than I can or need report here; the chief of them inevitably to the effect that my supposedly typical little figure was of course pure poetry, and had never been anything else; since this is what helpful imagin-ation, in however slight a dose, ever directly makes for. As for the original grossness of readers, I dare say I added, that was another matter – but one which at any rate had then quite ceased to signify.

HENRY JAMES

Daisy Miller

1

At the little town of Vevey,[3] in Switzerland, there is a
particularly comfortable hotel. There are, indeed, many
hotels; for the entertainment of tourists is the business
of the place, which, as many travellers will remember, is
seated upon the edge of a remarkably blue lake – a lake
that it behoves every tourist to visit. The shore of the
lake presents an unbroken array of establishments of this
order, of every category, from the 'grand hotel' of the
newest fashion, with a chalk-white front, a hundred bal-
conies, and a dozen flags flying from its roof, to the little
Swiss *pension*[4] of an elder day, with its name inscribed in
German-looking lettering upon a pink or yellow wall,
and an awkward summer-house in the angle of the
garden. One of the hotels at Vevey, however, is famous,
even classical, being distinguished from many of its
upstart neighbours by an air both of luxury and of matur-
ity. In this region, in the month of June, American travellers are extremely numerous; it may be said, indeed, that
Vevey assumes at this period some of the characteristics
of an American watering-place. There are sights and
sounds which evoke a vision, an echo, of Newport[5] and
Saratoga.[6] There is a flitting hither and thither of 'stylish'
young girls, a rustling of muslin flounces, a rattle of
dance-music in the morning hours, a sound of high-pit-
ched voices at all times. You receive an impression of these
things at the excellent inn of the Trois Couronnes,[7] and
are transported in fancy to the Ocean House[8] or to Congress Hall.[9] But at the Trois Couronnes, it must be added,

47

there are other features that are much at variance with
these suggestions: neat German waiters, who look like
secretaries of legation; Russian princesses sitting in the
garden; little Polish boys walking about, held by the
hand, with their governors; a view of the snowy crest of
the Dent du Midi[10] and the picturesque towers of the
Castle of Chillon.[11]

I hardly know whether it was the analogies or the diff-
erences that were uppermost in the mind of a young
American, who, two or three years ago, sat in the garden
of the Trois Couronnes, looking about him, rather idly,
at some of the graceful objects I have mentioned. It was
a beautiful summer morning, and in whatever fashion
the young American looked at things, they must have
seemed to him charming. He had come from Geneva[12]
the day before, by the little steamer, to see his aunt, who
was staying at the hotel – Geneva having been for a long
time his place of residence. But his aunt had a headache –
his aunt had almost always a headache – and now she
was shut up in her room, smelling camphor,[13] so that he
was at liberty to wander about. He was some seven-and-
twenty years of age; when his friends spoke of him, they
usually said that he was at Geneva, 'studying'. When his
enemies spoke of him they said – but, after all, he had
no enemies; he was an extremely amiable fellow, and
universally liked. What I should say is, simply, that
when certain persons spoke of him they affirmed that
the reason of his spending so much time at Geneva was
that he was extremely devoted to a lady who lived there –
a foreign lady – a person older than himself. Very few
Americans – indeed I think none – had ever seen this
lady, about whom there were some singular stories. But
Winterbourne had an old attachment for the little metropolis of Calvinism;[14] he had been put to school there as
a boy, and he had afterwards gone to college there –
circumstances which had led to his forming a great many

youthful friendships. Many of these he had kept, and they were a source of great satisfaction to him.

After knocking at his aunt's door and learning that she was indisposed, he had taken a walk about the town, and then he had come in to his breakfast. He had now finished his breakfast, but he was drinking a small cup of coffee, which had been served to him on a little table in the garden by one of the waiters who looked like an attaché.[15] At last he finished his coffee and lit a cigarette. Presently a small boy came walking along the path – an urchin of nine or ten. The child, who was diminutive for his years, had an aged expression of countenance, a pale complexion, and sharp little features. He was dressed in knickerbockers, with red stockings, which displayed his poor little spindleshanks;[16] he also wore a brilliant red cravat. He carried in his hand a long alpenstock,[17] the sharp point of which he thrust into everything that he approached – the flowerbeds, the garden-benches, the trains of the ladies' dresses. In front of Winterbourne he paused, looking at him with a pair of bright, penetrating little eyes.

'Will you give me a lump of sugar?' he asked, in a sharp, hard little voice – a voice immature, and yet, somehow, not young.

Winterbourne glanced at the small table near him, on which his coffee-service rested, and saw that several morsels of sugar remained. 'Yes, you may take one,' he answered; 'but I don't think sugar is good for little boys.'

This little boy stepped forward and carefully selected three of the coveted fragments, two of which he buried in the pocket of his knickerbockers, depositing the other as promptly in another place. He poked his alpenstock, lance-fashion, into Winterbourne's bench, and tried to crack the lump of sugar with his teeth.

'Oh, blazes; it's har-r-d!' he exclaimed, pronouncing the adjective in a peculiar manner.

Winterbourne had immediately perceived that he might have the honour of claiming him as a fellow-countryman. 'Take care you don't hurt your teeth,' he said, paternally.

'I haven't got any teeth to hurt. They have all come out. I have only got seven teeth. My mother counted them last night, and one came out right afterwards. She said she'd slap me if any more came out. I can't help it. It's this old Europe. It's the climate that makes them come out. In America they didn't come out. It's these hotels.'

Winterbourne was much amused. 'If you eat three lumps of sugar, your mother will certainly slap you,' he said.

'She's got to give me some candy, then,' rejoined his young interlocutor. 'I can't get any candy here – any American candy. American candy's the best candy.'

'And are American little boys the best little boys?' asked Winterbourne.

'I don't know. I'm an American boy,' said the child.

'I see you are one of the best!' laughed Winterbourne.

'Are you an American man?' pursued this vivacious infant. And then, on Winterbourne's affirmative reply – 'American men are the best,' he declared.

His companion thanked him for the compliment; and the child, who had now got astride of his alpenstock, stood looking about him, while he attacked a second lump of sugar. Winterbourne wondered if he himself had been like this in his infancy, for he had been brought to Europe at about this age.

'Here comes my sister!' cried the child, in a moment. 'She's an American girl.'

Winterbourne looked along the path and saw a beautiful young lady advancing. 'American girls are the best girls,' he said, cheerfully, to his young companion.

'My sister ain't the best!' the child declared. 'She's always blowing at me.'

'I imagine that is your fault, not hers,' said Winterbourne. The young lady meanwhile had drawn near. She was dressed in white muslin, with a hundred frills and flounces, and knots of pale-coloured ribbon. She was bare-headed; but she balanced in her hand a large parasol, with a deep border of embroidery; and she was strikingly, admirably pretty. 'How pretty they are!' thought Winterbourne, straightening himself in his seat, as if he were prepared to rise.

The young lady paused in front of his bench, near the parapet of the garden, which overlooked the lake. The little boy had now converted his alpenstock into a vaulting-pole, by the aid of which he was springing about in the gravel, and kicking it up not a little.

'Randolph,' said the young lady, 'what *are* you doing?'

'I'm going up the Alps,' replied Randolph. 'This is the way!' And he gave another little jump, scattering the pebbles about Winterbourne's ears.

'That's the way they come down,' said Winterbourne.

'He's an American man!' cried Randolph, in his little hard voice.

The young lady gave no heed to this announcement, but looked straight at her brother. 'Well, I guess you had better be quiet,' she simply observed.

It seemed to Winterbourne that he had been in a manner presented. He got up and stepped slowly towards the young girl, throwing away his cigarette. 'This little boy and I have made acquaintance,' he said, with great civility. In Geneva, as he had been perfectly aware, a young man was not at liberty to speak to a young unmarried lady except under certain rarely occurring conditions; but here, at Vevey, what conditions could be better than these? – a pretty American girl coming and standing in front of you in a garden. This pretty

American girl, however, on hearing Winterbourne's
observation, simply glanced at him; she then turned her
head and looked over the parapet, at the lake and the
opposite mountains. He wondered whether he had gone
too far; but he decided that he must advance farther
rather than retreat. While he was thinking of something
else to say, the young lady turned to the little boy again.

'I should like to know where you got that pole,' she
said.

'I bought it!' responded Randolph.

'You don't mean to say you're going to take it to Italy!'

'Yes, I am going to take it to Italy!' the child declared.

The young girl glanced over the front of her dress, and
smoothed out a knot or two of ribbon. Then she rested
her eyes upon the prospect again. 'Well, I guess you had
better leave it somewhere,' she said, after a moment.

'Are you going to Italy?' Winterbourne inquired, in a
tone of great respect.

The young lady glanced at him again. 'Yes, sir,' she
replied. And she said nothing more.

'Are you – a – going over the Simplon?'[18] Winterbourne pursued, a little embarrassed.

'I don't know,' she said. 'I suppose it's some mountain. Randolph, what mountain are we going over?'

'Going where?' the child demanded.

'To Italy,' Winterbourne explained.

'I don't know,' said Randolph. 'I don't want to go to
Italy. I want to go to America.'

'Oh, Italy is a beautiful place!' rejoined the young man.

'Can you get candy there?' Randolph loudly inquired.

'I hope not,' said his sister. 'I guess you have had
enough candy, and mother thinks so too.'

'I haven't had any for ever so long – for a hundred
weeks!' cried the boy, still jumping about.

The young lady inspected her flounces and smoothed
her ribbons again; and Winterbourne presently risked an

observation upon the beauty of the view. He was ceasing
to be embarrassed, for he had begun to perceive that she
was not in the least embarrassed herself. There had not
been the slightest alteration in her charming complexion;
she was evidently neither offended nor fluttered. If she
looked another way when he spoke to her, and seemed
not particularly to hear him, this was simply her habit,
her manner. Yet, as he talked a little more, and pointed
out some of the objects of interest in the view, with which
she appeared quite unacquainted, she gradually gave
him more of the benefit of her glance; and then he saw
that this glance was perfectly direct and unshrinking.
It was not, however, what would have been called an
immodest glance, for the young girl's eyes were singularly honest and fresh. They were wonderfully pretty
eyes; and, indeed, Winterbourne had not seen for a long
time anything prettier than his fair countrywoman's various features – her complexion, her nose, her ears, her
teeth. He had a great relish for feminine beauty; he was
addicted to observing and analysing it; and as regards
this young lady's face he made several observations. It
was not at all insipid, but it was not exactly expressive;
and though it was eminently delicate, Winterbourne
mentally accused it – very forgivingly – of a want of fin-
ish. He thought it very possible that Master Randolph's
sister was a coquette;[19] he was sure she had a spirit of
her own; but in her bright, sweet, superficial little visage
there was no mockery, no irony. Before long it became
obvious that she was much disposed towards conversation. She told him that they were going to Rome for the
winter – she and her mother and Randolph. She asked
him if he was a 'real American'; she wouldn't have taken
him for one; he seemed more like a German – this was
said after a little hesitation, especially when he spoke.
Winterbourne, laughing, answered that he had met Germans who spoke like Americans; but that he had not, so

far as he remembered, met an American who spoke like a German. Then he asked her if she would not be more comfortable in sitting upon the bench which he had just quitted. She answered that she liked standing up and walking about; but she presently sat down. She told him she was from New York State – 'if you know where that is'. Winterbourne learned more about her by catching hold of her small, slippery brother and making him stand a few minutes by his side.

'Tell me your name, my boy,' he said.

'Randolph C. Miller,' said the boy, sharply. 'And I'll tell you her name'; and he levelled his alpenstock at his sister.

'You had better wait till you are asked!' said this young lady, calmly.

'I should like very much to know your name,' said Winterbourne.

'Her name is Daisy Miller!'[20] cried the child. 'But that isn't her real name; that isn't her name on her cards.'

'It's a pity you haven't got one of my cards!' said Miss Miller.

'Her real name is Annie P. Miller,' the boy went on.

'Ask him *his* name,' said his sister, indicating Winterbourne.

But on this point Randolph seemed perfectly indifferent; he continued to supply information with regard to his own family. 'My father's name is Ezra B. Miller,' he announced. 'My father ain't in Europe; my father's in a better place than Europe.'

Winterbourne imagined for a moment that this was the manner in which the child had been taught to intimate that Mr Miller had been removed to the sphere of celestial rewards. But Randolph immediately added, 'My father's in Schenectady. He's got a big business. My father's rich, you bet.'

'Well!' ejaculated Miss Miller, lowering her parasol and

looking at the embroidered border. Winterbourne presently released the child, who departed, dragging his
alpenstock along the path. 'He doesn't like Europe,' said
the young girl. 'He wants to go back.'

'To Schenectady, you mean?'

'Yes; he wants to go right home. He hasn't got any
boys here. There is one boy here, but he always goes
round with a teacher; they won't let him play.'

'And your brother hasn't any teacher?' Winterbourne
inquired.

'Mother thought of getting him one, to travel round
with us. There was a lady told her of a very good teacher;
an American lady – perhaps you know her – Mrs San-
ders. I think she came from Boston. She told her of this
teacher, and we thought of getting him to travel round
with us. But Randolph said he didn't want a teacher
travelling round with us. He said he wouldn't have lessons when he was in the cars.[21] And we *are* in the cars
about half the time. There was an English lady we met
in the cars – I think her name was Miss Featherstone;
perhaps you know her. She wanted to know why I didn't
give Randolph lessons – give him "instruction", she
called it. I guess he could give me more instruction than
I could give him. He's very smart.'

'Yes,' said Winterbourne; 'he seems very smart.'

'Mother's going to get a teacher for him as soon as we
get to Italy. Can you get good teachers in Italy?'

'Very good, I should think,' said Winterbourne.

'Or else she's going to find some school. He ought to
learn some more. He's only nine. He's going to college.'
And in this way Miss Miller continued to converse upon
the affairs of her family, and upon other topics. She sat
there with her extremely pretty hands, ornamented with
very brilliant rings, folded in her lap, and with her pretty
eyes now resting upon those of Winterbourne, now
wandering over the garden, the people who passed by,

and the beautiful view. She talked to Winterbourne as if she had known him a long time. He found it very pleasant. It was many years since he had heard a young girl talk so much. It might have been said of this unknown young lady, who had come and sat down beside him upon a bench, that she chattered. She was very quiet, she sat in a charming tranquil attitude; but her lips and her eyes were constantly moving. She had a soft, slender, agreeable voice, and her tone was decidedly sociable. She gave Winterbourne a history of her movements and intentions, and those of her mother and brother, in Europe, and enumerated, in particular, the various hotels at which they had stopped. 'That English lady in the cars,' she said – 'Miss Featherstone – asked me if we didn't all live in hotels in America. I told her I had never been in so many hotels in my life as since I came to Europe. I have never seen so many – it's nothing but hotels.' But Miss Miller did not make this remark with a querulous accent; she appeared to be in the best humour with everything. She declared that the hotels were very good, when once you got used to their ways, and that Europe was perfectly sweet. She was not disappointed – not a bit. Perhaps it was because she had heard so much about it before. She had ever so many[22] intimate friends that had been there ever so many times. And then she had had ever so many dresses and things from Paris. Whenever she put on a Paris dress she felt as if she were in Europe.

'It was a kind of wishing-cap,' said Winterbourne.

'Yes,' said Miss Miller, without examining this analogy; 'it always made me wish I was here. But I needn't have done that for dresses. I am sure they send all the pretty ones to America; you see the most frightful things here. The only thing I don't like,' she proceeded, 'is the society. There isn't any society; or, if there is, I don't know where it keeps itself. Do you? I suppose there is

some society somewhere, but I haven't seen anything of
it. I'm very fond of society, and I have always had a great
deal of it. I don't mean only in Schenectady, but in New
York. I used to go to New York every winter. In New
York I had lots of society. Last winter I had seventeen
dinners given me; and three of them were by gentlemen,'
added Daisy Miller. 'I have more friends in New York
than in Schenectady – more gentlemen friends, and more
young lady friends too,' she resumed in a moment. She
paused again for an instant; she was looking at Winterbourne with all her prettiness in her lively eyes and in
her light, slightly monotonous smile. 'I have always
had,' she said, 'a great deal of gentlemen's society.'

Poor Winterbourne was amused, perplexed, and
decidedly charmed. He had never yet heard a young girl
express herself in just this fashion; never, at least, save
in cases where to say such things seemed a kind of
demonstrative evidence of a certain laxity of deportment.
And yet was he to accuse Miss Daisy Miller of actual or
potential *inconduite*,[23] as they said at Geneva? He felt that
he had lived at Geneva so long that he had lost a good
deal; he had become dishabituated to the American tone.
Never, indeed, since he had grown old enough to appreciate things, had he encountered a young American girl
of so pronounced a type as this. Certainly she was very
charming; but how deucedly sociable! Was she simply a
pretty girl from New York State – were they all like that,
the pretty girls who had a good deal of gentlemen's society? Or was she also a designing, an audacious, an
unscrupulous young person? Winterbourne had lost his
instinct in this matter, and his reason could not help him.
Miss Daisy Miller looked extremely innocent. Some
people had told him that, after all, American girls were
exceedingly innocent; and others had told him that, after
all, they were not. He was inclined to think Miss Daisy
Miller was a flirt[24] – a pretty American flirt. He had never,

as yet, had any relations with young ladies of this category. He had known, here in Europe, two or three
women – persons older than Miss Daisy Miller, and provided, for respectability's sake, with husbands – who
were great coquettes – dangerous, terrible women, with
whom one's relations were liable to take a serious turn.
But this young girl was not a coquette in that sense; she
was very unsophisticated; she was only a pretty American flirt. Winterbourne was almost grateful for having
found the formula that applied to Miss Daisy Miller. He
leaned back in his seat; he remarked to himself that she
had the most charming nose he had ever seen; he wondered what were the regular conditions and limitations
of one's intercourse with a pretty American flirt. It presently became apparent that he was on the way to learn.

'Have you been to that old castle?' asked the young
girl, pointing with her parasol to the far-gleaming walls
of the Château de Chillon.

'Yes, formerly, more than once,' said Winterbourne.
'You too, I suppose, have seen it?'

'No; we haven't been there. I want to go there dreadfully. Of course I mean to go there. I wouldn't go away
from here without having seen that old castle.'

'It's a very pretty excursion,' said Winterbourne, 'and
very easy to make. You can drive, you know, or you can
go by the little steamer.'

'You can go in the cars,' said Miss Miller.

'Yes; you can go in the cars,' Winterbourne assented.

'Our courier[25] says they take you right up to the castle,'
the young girl continued. 'We were going last week; but
my mother gave out. She suffers dreadfully from
dyspepsia. She said she couldn't go. Randolph wouldn't
go either; he says he doesn't think much of old castles.
But I guess we'll go this week, if we can get Randolph.'

'Your brother is not interested in ancient monuments?'
Winterbourne inquired, smiling.

'He says he don't care much about old castles. He's
only nine. He wants to stay at the hotel. Mother's afraid
to leave him alone, and the courier won't stay with him;
so we haven't been to many places. But it will be too bad
if we don't go up there.' And Miss Miller pointed again
at the Château de Chillon.

'I should think it might be arranged,' said Winterbourne. 'Couldn't you get someone to stay – for the afternoon – with Randolph?'

Miss Miller looked at him a moment; and then, very
placidly – 'I wish *you* would stay with him!' she said.

Winterbourne hesitated a moment. 'I would much
rather go to Chillon with you.'

'With me?' asked the young girl, with the same placid-
ity.

She didn't rise, blushing, as a young girl at Geneva
would have done; and yet Winterbourne, conscious that
he had been very bold, thought it possible she was
offended. 'With your mother,' he answered very respect-
fully.

But it seemed that both his audacity and his respect
were lost upon Miss Daisy Miller. 'I guess my mother
won't go, after all,' she said. 'She don't like to ride round
in the afternoon. But did you really mean what you said
just now; that you would like to go up there?'

'Most earnestly,' Winterbourne declared.

'Then we may arrange it. If mother will stay with Randolph, I guess Eugenio will.'

'Eugenio?' the young man inquired.

'Eugenio's our courier. He doesn't like to stay with
Randolph; he's the most fastidious man I ever saw. But
he's a splendid courier. I guess he'll stay at home with
Randolph if mother does, and then we can go to the
castle.'

Winterbourne reflected for an instant as lucidly as
possible – 'we' could only mean Miss Daisy Miller and

himself. This programme seemed almost too agreeable for credence; he felt as if he ought to kiss the young lady's hand. Possibly he would have done so – and quite spoiled the project; but at this moment another person – presumably Eugenio – appeared. A tall, handsome man, with superb whiskers, wearing a velvet morning-coat and a brilliant watch-chain, approached Miss Miller, looking sharply at her companion. 'Oh, Eugenio!' said Miss Miller, with the friendliest accent.

Eugenio had looked at Winterbourne from head to foot, he now bowed gravely to the young lady. 'I have the honour to inform mademoiselle that luncheon is upon the table.'

Miss Miller slowly rose. 'See here, Eugenio,' she said. 'I'm going to that old castle, anyway.'

'To the Château de Chillon, mademoiselle?' the courier inquired. 'Mademoiselle has made arrangements?' he added, in a tone which struck Winterbourne as very impertinent.

Eugenio's tone apparently threw, even to Miss Miller's own apprehension, a slightly ironical light upon the young girl's situation. She turned to Winterbourne, blushing a little – a very little. 'You won't back out?' she said.

'I shall not be happy till we go!' he protested.

'And you are staying in this hotel?' she went on. 'And you are really an American?'

The courier stood looking at Winterbourne, offensively. The young man, at least, thought his manner of looking an offence to Miss Miller; it conveyed an imputation that she 'picked up' acquaintances. 'I shall have the honour of presenting to you a person who will tell you all about me,' he said smiling, and referring to his aunt.

'Oh well, we'll go some day,' said Miss Miller. And she gave him a smile and turned away. She put up her parasol and walked back to the inn beside Eugenio.

Winterbourne stood looking after her; and as she moved
away, drawing her muslin furbelows[26] over the gravel,
said to himself that she had the *tournure*[27] of a princess.

2

He had, however, engaged to do more than proved feas-
ible, in promising to present his aunt, Mrs Costello, to
Miss Daisy Miller. As soon as the former lady had got
better of her headache he waited upon her in her apartment; and, after the proper inquiries in regard to her
health, he asked her if she had observed, in the hotel, an
American family – a mamma, a daughter, and a little boy.

'And a courier?' said Mrs Costello. 'Oh, yes, I have
observed them. Seen them – heard them – and kept out
of their way.' Mrs Costello was a widow with a fortune;
a person of much distinction, who frequently intimated
that, if she were not so dreadfully liable to sick-head-
aches, she would probably have left a deeper impress
upon her time. She had a long pale face, a high nose,
and a great deal of very striking white hair, which she
wore in large puffs and *rouleaux*[28] over the top of her
head. She had two sons married in New York, and
another who was now in Europe. This young man was
amusing himself at Homburg, and, though he was on
his travels, was rarely perceived to visit any particular
city at the moment selected by his mother for her own
appearance there. Her nephew, who had come up to
Vevey expressly to see her, was therefore more attentive
than those who, as she said, were nearer to her. He had
imbibed at Geneva the idea that one must always be
attentive to one's aunt. Mrs Costello had not seen him

for many years, and she was greatly pleased with him, manifesting her approbation by initiating him into many of the secrets of that social sway which, as she gave him to understand, she exerted in the American capital. She admitted that she was very exclusive; but, if he were acquainted with New York, he would see that one had to be. And her picture of the minutely hierarchical constitution of the society of that city, which she presented to him in many different lights, was, to Winterbourne's imagination, almost oppressively striking.

He immediately perceived, from her tone, that Miss Daisy Miller's place in the social scale was low. 'I am afraid you don't approve of them,' he said.

'They are very common,' Mrs Costello declared. 'They are the sort of Americans that one does one's duty by not – not accepting.'

'Ah, you don't accept them?' said the young man.

'I can't, my dear Frederick. I would if I could, but I can't.'

'The young girl is very pretty,' said Winterbourne, in a moment.

'Of course she's pretty. But she is very common.'

'I see what you mean, of course,' said Winterbourne, after another pause.

'She has that charming look that they all have,' his aunt resumed. 'I can't think where they pick it up; and she dresses in perfection – no, you don't know how well she dresses. I can't think where they get their taste.'

'But, my dear aunt, she is not, after all, a Comanche savage.'

'She is a young lady,' said Mrs Costello, 'who has an intimacy with her mamma's courier.'

'An intimacy with the courier?' the young man demanded.

'Oh, the mother is just as bad! They treat the courier

like a familiar friend – like a gentleman. I shouldn't wonder if he dines with them. Very likely they have never seen a man with such good manners, such fine clothes, so like a gentleman. He probably corresponds to the young lady's idea of a Count. He sits with them in the garden, in the evening. I think he smokes.'

Winterbourne listened with interest to these disclosures; they helped him to make up his mind about Miss Daisy. Evidently she was rather wild. 'Well,' he said, 'I am not a courier, and yet she was very charming to me.'

'You had better have said at first,' said Mrs Costello with dignity, 'that you had made her acquaintance.'

'We simply met in the garden, and we talked a bit.'

'*Tout bonnement!*[29] And pray what did you say?'

'I said I should take the liberty of introducing her to my admirable aunt.'

'I am much obliged to you.'

'It was to guarantee my respectability,' said Winterbourne.

'And pray who is to guarantee hers?'

'Ah, you are cruel!' said the young man. 'She's a very nice girl.'

'You don't say that as if you believed it,' Mrs Costello observed.

'She is completely uncultivated,' Winterbourne went on. 'But she is wonderfully pretty, and, in short, she is very nice. To prove that I believe it, I am going to take her to the Château de Chillon.'

'You two are going off there together? I should say it proved just the contrary. How long had you known her, may I ask, when this interesting project was formed? You haven't been twenty-four hours in the house.'

'I had known her half an hour!' said Winterbourne, smiling.

'Dear me!' cried Mrs Costello. 'What a dreadful girl!'

Her nephew was silent for some moments. 'You really

think, then,' he began earnestly, and with a desire for
trustworthy information – 'you really think that –' But he
paused again.

'Think what, sir,' said his aunt.

'That she is the sort of young lady who expects a man –
sooner or later – to carry her off?'

'I haven't the least idea what such young ladies expect
a man to do. But I really think that you had better not
meddle with little American girls that are uncultivated,
as you call them. You have lived too long out of the
country. You will be sure to make some great mistake.
You are too innocent.'

'My dear aunt, I am not so innocent,' said Winterbourne, smiling and curling his moustache.

'You are too guilty, then?'

Winterbourne continued to curl his moustache, medi-
tatively. 'You won't let the poor girl know you then?' he
asked at last.

'Is it literally true that she is going to the Château de
Chillon with you?'

'I think that she fully intends it.'

'Then, my dear Frederick,' said Mrs Costello, 'I must
decline the honour of her acquaintance. I am an old
woman, but I am not too old – thank Heaven – to be
shocked!'

'But don't they all do these things – the young girls in
America?' Winterbourne inquired.

Mrs Costello stared a moment. 'I should like to see my
grand-daughters do them!' she declared, grimly.

This seemed to throw some light upon the matter, for
Winterbourne remembered to have heard that his pretty
cousins in New York were 'tremendous flirts'. If, therefore, Miss Daisy Miller exceeded the liberal licence
allowed to these young ladies, it was probable that anything might be expected of her. Winterbourne was impatient to see her again, and he was vexed with himself

that, by instinct, he should not appreciate her justly.

Though he was impatient to see her, he hardly knew what he should say to her about his aunt's refusal to become acquainted with her; but he discovered, promptly enough, that with Miss Daisy Miller there was no great need of walking on tiptoe. He found her that evening in the garden, wandering about in the warm starlight, like an indolent sylph, and swinging to and fro the largest fan he had ever beheld. It was ten o'clock. He had dined with his aunt, had been sitting with her since dinner, and had just taken leave of her till the morrow. Miss Daisy Miller seemed very glad to see him; she declared it was the longest evening she had ever passed.

'Have you been all alone?' he asked.

'I have been walking round with mother. But mother gets tired walking round,' she answered.

'Has she gone to bed?'

'No; she doesn't like to go to bed,' said the young girl. 'She doesn't sleep – not three hours. She says she doesn't know how she lives. She's dreadfully nervous. I guess she sleeps more than she thinks. She's gone somewhere after Randolph; she wants to try to get him to go to bed. He doesn't like to go to bed.'

'Let us hope she will persuade him,' observed Winterbourne.

'She will talk to him all she can; but he doesn't like her to talk to him,' said Miss Daisy, opening her fan. 'She's going to try to get Eugenio to talk to him. But he isn't afraid of Eugenio. Eugenio's a splendid courier, but he can't make much impression on Randolph! I don't believe he'll go to bed before eleven.' It appeared that Randolph's vigil was in fact triumphantly prolonged, for Winterbourne strolled about with the young girl for some time without meeting her mother. 'I have been looking round for that lady you want to introduce me to,' his companion resumed. 'She's your aunt.' Then, on Winterbourne's admitting the fact, and expressing some curiosity as to how she had learned it, she said she had heard all about Mrs Costello from the chambermaid. She was very quiet and very *comme il faut*;[30] she wore white puffs; she spoke to no one, and she never dined at the *table d'hôte*.[31] Every two days she had a headache. 'I think that's a lovely description, headache and all!' said Miss Daisy, chattering along in her thin, gay voice. 'I want to know her ever so much. I know just what *your* aunt would be; I know I should like her. She would be very exclusive. I like a lady to be exclusive; I'm dying to be exclusive myself. Well, we *are* exclusive, mother and I. We don't speak to everyone – or they don't speak to us. I suppose it's about the same thing. Anyway, I shall be ever so glad to know your aunt.'

Winterbourne was embarrassed. 'She would be most happy,' he said, 'but I am afraid those headaches will interfere.'

The young girl looked at him through the dusk. 'But I suppose she doesn't have a headache every day,' she said, sympathetically.

Winterbourne was silent a moment. 'She tells me she does,' he answered at last – not knowing what to say.

Miss Daisy Miller stopped and stood looking at him. Her prettiness was still visible in the darkness; she was opening and closing her enormous fan. 'She doesn't want to know me!' she said suddenly. 'Why don't you say so? You needn't be afraid. I'm not afraid!' And she gave a little laugh.

Winterbourne fancied there was a tremor in her voice; he was touched, shocked, mortified by it. 'My dear young lady,' he protested, 'she knows no one. It's her wretched health.'

The young girl walked on a few steps, laughing still. 'You needn't be afraid,' she repeated. 'Why should she want to know me?' Then she paused again; she was close to the parapet of the garden, and in front of her was the starlit lake. There was a vague sheen upon its surface, and in the distance were dimly seen mountain forms. Daisy Miller looked out upon the mysterious prospect, and then she gave another little laugh. 'Gracious! she *is* exclusive!' she said. Winterbourne wondered whether she was seriously wounded, and for a moment almost wished that her sense of injury might be such as to make it becoming in him to attempt to reassure and comfort her. He had a pleasant sense that she would be very approachable for consolatory purposes. He felt then, for the instant, quite ready to sacrifice his aunt, conversationally; to admit that she was a proud, rude woman, and to declare that they needn't mind her. But before he had time to commit himself to this perilous mixture of gallantry and impiety, the young lady, resuming her walk, gave an exclamation in quite another tone. 'Well; here's mother! I guess she hasn't got Randolph to go to bed.' The figure of a lady appeared, at a distance, very indistinct in the darkness, and advancing with a slow and wavering movement. Suddenly it seemed to pause.

'Are you sure it is your mother? Can you distinguish her in this thick dusk?' Winterbourne asked.

'Well!' cried Miss Daisy Miller, with a laugh, 'I guess I know my own mother. And when she has got on my shawl, too! She is always wearing my things.'

The lady in question, ceasing to advance, hovered vaguely about the spot at which she had checked her steps.

'I am afraid your mother doesn't see you,' said Winterbourne. 'Or perhaps,' he added – thinking, with Miss Miller, the joke permissible – 'perhaps she feels guilty about your shawl.'

'Oh, it's a fearful old thing!' the young girl replied,

serenely. 'I told her she could wear it. She won't come here, because she sees you.'

'Ah, then,' said Winterbourne, 'I had better leave you.'

'Oh, no; come on!' urged Miss Daisy Miller.

'I'm afraid your mother doesn't approve of my walking with you.'

Miss Miller gave him a serious glance. 'It isn't for me; it's for you – that is, it's for *her*. Well; I don't know who it's for! But mother doesn't like any of my gentlemen friends. She's right down timid. She always makes a fuss if I introduce a gentleman. But I *do* introduce them – almost always. If I didn't introduce my gentlemen friends to mother,' the young girl added, in her little soft, flat monotone, 'I shouldn't think I was natural.'

'To introduce me,' said Winterbourne, 'you must know my name.' And he proceeded to pronounce it.

'Oh, dear; I can't say all that!' said his companion, with a laugh. But by this time they had come up to Mrs Miller, who, as they drew near, walked to the parapet of the garden and leaned upon it, looking intently at the lake and turning her back upon them. 'Mother!' said the young girl, in a tone of decision. Upon this the elder lady turned round. 'Mr Winterbourne,' said Miss Daisy Miller, introducing the young man very frankly and prettily. 'Common' she was, as Mrs Costello had pronounced her; yet it was a wonder to Winterbourne that, with her commonness, she had a singularly delicate grace.

Her mother was a small, spare, light person, with a wandering eye, a very exiguous nose, and a large forehead, decorated with a certain amount of thin, much-frizzled hair. Like her daughter, Mrs Miller was dressed with extreme elegance; she had enormous diamonds in her ears. So far as Winterbourne could observe, she gave him no greeting – she certainly was not looking at him. Daisy was near her, pulling her shawl straight. 'What are you doing, poking round here?' this young lady inquired; but by no means with that harshness of accent which her choice of words may imply.

'I don't know,' said her mother, turning towards the lake again.

'I shouldn't think you'd want that shawl!' Daisy exclaimed.

'Well – I do!' her mother answered, with a little laugh.

'Did you get Randolph to go to bed?' asked the young girl.

'No; I couldn't induce him,' said Mrs Miller, very gently. 'He wants to talk to the waiter. He likes to talk to that waiter.'

'I was telling Mr Winterbourne,' the young girl went on; and to the young man's ear her tone might have indicated that she had been uttering his name all her life.

'Oh yes!' said Winterbourne; 'I have the pleasure of knowing your son.'

Randolph's mamma was silent; she turned her attention to the lake. But at last she spoke. 'Well, I don't see how he lives!'

'Anyhow, it isn't so bad as it was at Dover,' said Daisy Miller.

'And what occurred at Dover?' Winterbourne asked.

'He wouldn't go to bed at all. I guess he sat up all night – in the public parlour. He wasn't in bed at twelve o'clock: I know that.'

'It was half past twelve,' declared Mrs Miller, with mild emphasis.

'Does he sleep much during the day?' Winterbourne demanded.

'I guess he doesn't sleep much,' Daisy rejoined.

'I wish he would!' said her mother. 'It seems as if he couldn't.'

'I think he's real tiresome,' Daisy pursued.

Then, for some moments, there was silence. 'Well,

Daisy Miller,' said the elder lady, presently, 'I shouldn't think you'd want to talk against your own brother!'

'Well, he *is* tiresome, mother,' said Daisy, quite without the asperity of a retort.

'He's only nine,' urged Mrs Miller.

'Well, he wouldn't go to that castle,' said the young girl. 'I'm going there with Mr Winterbourne.'

To this announcement, very placidly made, Daisy's mamma offered no response. Winterbourne took for granted that she deeply disapproved of the projected excursion; but he said to himself that she was a simple, easily managed person, and that a few deferential protestations would take the edge from her displeasure. 'Yes,' he began; 'your daughter has kindly allowed me the honour of being her guide.'

Mrs Miller's wandering eyes attached themselves, with a sort of appealing air, to Daisy, who, however, strolled a few steps farther, gently humming to herself. 'I presume you will go in the cars,' said her mother.

'Yes; or in the boat,' said Winterbourne.

'Well, of course, I don't know,' Mrs Miller rejoined. 'I have never been to that castle.'

'It is a pity you shouldn't go,' said Winterbourne, beginning to feel reassured as to her opposition. And yet he was quite prepared to find that, as a matter of course, she meant to accompany her daughter.

'We've been thinking ever so much about going,' she pursued; 'but it seems as if we couldn't. Of course Daisy – she wants to go round. But there's a lady here – I don't know her name – she says she shouldn't think we'd want to go to see castles *here*; she should think we'd want to wait till we got to Italy. It seems as if there would be so many there,' continued Mrs Miller, with an air of increasing confidence. 'Of course, we only want to see the principal ones. We visited several in England,' she presently added.

'Ah yes! in England there are beautiful castles,' said Winterbourne. 'But Chillon, here, is very well worth seeing.'

'Well, if Daisy feels up to it –,' said Mrs Miller, in a tone impregnated with a sense of the magnitude of the enterprise. 'It seems as if there was nothing she wouldn't undertake.'

'Oh, I think she'll enjoy it!' Winterbourne declared. And he desired more and more to make it a certainty that he was to have the privilege of a *tête-à-tête* with the young lady, who was still strolling along in front of them, softly vocalizing. 'You are not disposed, madam,' he inquired, 'to undertake it yourself?'

Daisy's mother looked at him, an instant, askance, and then walked forward in silence. Then – 'I guess she had better go along,' she said, simply.

Winterbourne observed to himself that this was a very different type of maternity from that of the vigilant matrons who massed themselves in the forefront of social intercourse in the dark old city at the other end of the lake.[32] But his meditations were interrupted by hearing his name very distinctly pronounced by Mrs Miller's unprotected daughter.

'Mr Winterbourne!' murmured Daisy.

'Mademoiselle!' said the young man.

'Don't you want to take me out in a boat?'

'At present?' he asked.

'Of course!' said Daisy.

'Well, Annie Miller!' exclaimed her mother.

'I beg you, madam, to let her go,' said Winterbourne, ardently; for he had never yet enjoyed the sensation of guiding through the summer starlight a skiff freighted with a fresh and beautiful young girl.

'I shouldn't think she'd want to,' said her mother. 'I should think she'd rather go indoors.'

'I'm sure Mr Winterbourne wants to take me,' Daisy declared. 'He's so awfully devoted!'

'I will row you over to Chillon, in the starlight.'

'I don't believe it!' said Daisy.

'Well!' ejaculated the elder lady again.

'You haven't spoken to me for half an hour,' her daughter went on.

'I have been having some very pleasant conversation with your mother,' said Winterbourne.

'Well; I want you to take me out in a boat!' Daisy repeated. They had all stopped, and she turned round and was looking at Winterbourne. Her face wore a charming smile, her pretty eyes were gleaming, she was swinging her great fan about. No; it's impossible to be prettier than that, thought Winterbourne.

'There are half a dozen boats moored at that landing-place,' he said, pointing to certain steps which descended from the garden to the lake. 'If you will do me the honour to accept my arm, we will go and select one of them.'

Daisy stood there smiling; she threw back her head and gave a little light laugh. 'I like a gentleman to be formal!' she declared.

'I assure you it's a formal offer.'

'I was bound I would make you say something,' Daisy went on.

'You see it's not very difficult,' said Winterbourne. 'But I am afraid you are chaffing[33] me.'

'I think not, sir,' remarked Mrs Miller, very gently.

'Do, then, let me give you a row,' he said to the young girl.

'It's quite lovely, the way you say that!' cried Daisy.

'It will be still more lovely to do it.'

'Yes, it would be lovely!' said Daisy. But she made no movement to accompany him; she only stood there laughing.

'I should think you had better find out what time it is,' interposed her mother.

'It is eleven o'clock, madam,' said a voice, with a foreign accent, out of the neighbouring darkness; and Winterbourne, turning, perceived the florid personage who was in attendance upon the two ladies. He had apparently just approached.

'Oh, Eugenio,' said Daisy, 'I am going out in a boat!'

Eugenio bowed. 'At eleven o'clock, mademoiselle?'

'I am going with Mr Winterbourne. This very minute.'

'Do tell her she can't,' said Mrs Miller to the courier.

'I think you had better not go out in a boat, mademoiselle,' Eugenio declared.

Winterbourne wished to Heaven this pretty girl were not so familiar with her courier; but he said nothing.

'I suppose you don't think it's proper!' Daisy exclaimed, 'Eugenio doesn't think anything's proper.'

'I am at your service,' said Winterbourne.

'Does mademoiselle propose to go alone?' asked Eugenio of Mrs Miller.

'Oh, no; with this gentleman!' answered Daisy's mamma.

The courier looked for a moment at Winterbourne – the latter thought he was smiling – and then, solemnly, with a bow, 'As mademoiselle pleases!' he said.

'Oh, I hoped you would make a fuss!' said Daisy. 'I don't care to go now.'

'I myself shall make a fuss if you don't go,' said Winterbourne.

'That's all I want – a little fuss!' And the young girl began to laugh again.

'Mr Randolph has gone to bed!' the courier announced, frigidly.

'Oh, Daisy; now we can go!' said Mrs Miller.

Daisy turned away from Winterbourne, looking at him, smiling and fanning herself. 'Good night,' she said;

'I hope you are disappointed, or disgusted, or something!'

He looked at her, taking the hand she offered him. 'I
am puzzled,' he answered.

'Well; I hope it won't keep you awake!' she said, very
smartly; and, under the escort of the privileged Eugenio,
the two ladies passed towards the house.

Winterbourne stood looking after them; he was indeed
puzzled. He lingered beside the lake for a quarter of an
hour, turning over the mystery of the young girl's
sudden familiarities and caprices. But the only very
definite conclusion he came to was that he should enjoy
deucedly 'going off' with her somewhere.

Two days afterwards he went off with her to the Castle
of Chillon. He waited for her in the large hall of the hotel,
where the couriers, the servants, the foreign tourists
were lounging about and staring. It was not the place he
would have chosen, but she had appointed it. She came
tripping downstairs, buttoning her long gloves, squeezing her folded parasol against her pretty figure, dressed
in the perfection of a soberly elegant travelling-costume.
Winterbourne was a man of imagination and, as our
ancestors used to say, of sensibility; as he looked at her
dress and, on the great staircase, her little rapid, confid-
ing step, he felt as if there were something romantic going
forward. He could have believed he was going to elope
with her. He passed out with her among all the idle
people that were assembled there; they were all lookin~
at her very hard; she had begun to chatter as soon as
she joined him. Winterbourne's preference had been that
they should be conveyed to Chillon in a carriage; but she
expressed a lively wish to go in the little steamer; she
declared that she had a passion for steamboats. There
was always such a lovely breeze upon the water, and
you saw such lots of people. The sail was not long, but
Winterbourne's companion found time to say a great

many things. To the young man himself their little excursion was so much of an escapade – an adventure – that, even allowing for her habitual sense of freedom, he had some expectation of seeing her regard it in the same way. But it must be confessed that, in this particular, he was disappointed. Daisy Miller was extremely animated, she was in charming spirits; but she was apparently not at all excited; she was not fluttered; she avoided neither his eyes nor those of anyone else; she blushed neither when she looked at him nor when she saw that people were looking at her. People continued to look at her a great deal, and Winterbourne took much satisfaction in his pretty companion's distinguished air. He had been a little afraid that she would talk loud, laugh overmuch, and even, perhaps, desire to move about the boat a good deal. But he quite forgot his fears; he sat smiling, with his eyes upon her face, while without moving from her place, she delivered herself of a great number of original reflections. It was the most charming garrulity he had ever heard. He had assented to the idea that she was 'common'; but was she so, after all, or was he simply getting used to her commonness? Her conversation was chiefly of what metaphysicians term the objective cast;[34] but every now and then it took a subjective turn.

'What on *earth* are you so grave about?' she suddenly demanded, fixing her agreeable eyes upon Winterbourne's.

'Am I grave?' he asked. 'I had an idea I was grinning from ear to ear.'

'You look as if you were taking me to a funeral.[35] If that's a grin, your ears are very near together.'

'Should you like me to dance a hornpipe on the deck?'

'Pray do, and I'll carry round your hat. It will pay the expenses of our journey.'

'I never was better pleased in my life,' murmured Winterbourne.

She looked at him a moment, and then burst into a little laugh. 'I like to make you say those things! You're a queer mixture!'

In the castle, after they had landed, the subjective element decidedly prevailed. Daisy tripped about the vaulted chambers, rustled her skirts in the corkscrew staircases, flirted[36] back with a pretty little cry and a shudder from the edge of the *oubliettes*,[37] and turned a singularly well-shaped ear to everything that Winterbourne told her about the place. But he saw that she cared very little for feudal antiquities, and that the dusky traditions of Chillon made but a slight impression upon her. They had the good fortune to have been able to walk about without other companionship than that of the custodian; and Winterbourne arranged with this functionary that they should not be hurried – that they should linger and pause wherever they chose. The custodian interpreted the bargain generously – Winterbourne, on his side, had been generous – and ended by leaving them quite to themselves. Miss Miller's observations were not remarkable for logical consistency; for anything she wanted to say she was sure to find a pretext. She found a great many pretexts in the rugged embrasures of Chillon for asking Winterbourne sudden questions about himself – his family, his previous history, his tastes, his habits, his intentions – and for supplying information upon corresponding points in her own personality. Of her own tastes, habits, and intentions Miss Miller was prepared to give the most definite, and indeed the most favourable, account.

'Well; I hope you know enough!' she said to her companion, after he had told her the history of the unhappy Bonnivard.[38] 'I never saw a man that knew so much!' The history of Bonnivard had evidently, as they say, gone one ear and out of the other. But Daisy went on to say that she wished Winterbourne would travel with them and 'go round' with them; they might know something, in that case. 'Don't you want to come and teach Randolph?' she asked. Winterbourne said that nothing could possibly please him so much; but that he had unfortunately other occupations. 'Other occupations? I don't believe it!' said Miss Daisy. 'What do you mean? You are not in business.' The young man admitted that he was not in business; but he had engagements which, even within a day or two, would force him to go back to Geneva. 'Oh, bother!' she said, 'I don't believe it!' and she began to talk about something else. But a few moments later, when he was pointing out to her the pretty design of an antique fireplace, she broke out irrelevantly, 'You don't mean to say you are going back to Geneva?'

'It is a melancholy fact that I shall have to return to Geneva tomorrow.'

'Well, Mr Winterbourne,' said Daisy; 'I think you're horrid!'

'Oh, don't say such dreadful things!' said Winterbourne, 'just at the last.'

'The last!' cried the young girl; 'I call it the first. I have half a mind to leave you here and go straight back to the hotel alone.' And for the nex' ten minutes she did nothing but call him horrid. Poor Winterbourne was fairly bewildered; no young lady had as yet done him the honour to be so agitated by the announcement of his movements. His companion, after this, ceased to pay any attention to the curiosities of Chillon or the beauties of the lake; she opened fire upon the mysterious charmer in Geneva, whom she appeared to have instantly taken it for granted that he was hurrying back to see. How did Miss Daisy Miller know that there was a charmer in Geneva? Winterbourne, who denied the existence of such a person, was quite unable to discover; and he was

divided between amazement at the rapidity of her induc-
tion and amusement at the frankness of her *persiflage*.[39]
She seemed to him, in all this, an extraordinary mixture
of innocence and crudity. 'Does she never allow you
more than three days at a time?' asked Daisy, ironically.
'Doesn't she give you a vacation in summer? There's no
one so hard worked but they can get leave to go off somewhere at this season. I suppose, if you stay another day,
she'll come after you in the boat. Do wait over till Friday,
and I will go down to the landing to see her arrive!'
Winterbourne began to think he had been wrong to feel
disappointed in the temper in which the young lady had
embarked. If he had missed the personal accent, the personal accent was now making its appearance. It sounded
very distinctly, at last, in her telling him she would stop
'teasing' him if he would promise her solemnly to come
down to Rome in the winter.

'That's not a difficult promise to make,' said Winterbourne. 'My aunt has taken an apartment in Rome for
the winter, and has already asked me to come and see
her.'

'I don't want you to come for your aunt,' said Daisy; 'I
want you to come for me.' And this was the only allusion
that the young man was ever to hear her make to his
invidious[40] kinswoman. He declared that, at any rate, he
would certainly come. After this Daisy stopped teasing.
Winterbourne took a carriage, and they drove back to
Vevey in the dusk; the young girl was very quiet.

In the evening Winterbourne mentioned to Mrs
Costello that he had spent the afternoon at Chillon, with
Miss Daisy Miller.

'The Americans – of the courier?' asked this lady.

'Ah, happily,' said Winterbourne, 'the courier stayed
at home.'

'She went with you all alone?'

'All alone.'

Mrs Costello sniffed a little at her smelling-bottle. 'And that,' she exclaimed, 'is the young person you wanted me to know!'

3

Winterbourne, who had returned to Geneva the day after his excursion to Chillon, went to Rome towards the end of January. His aunt had been established there for several weeks, and he had received a couple of letters from her. 'Those people you were so devoted to last summer at Vevey have turned up here, courier and all,' she wrote. 'They seem to have made several acquaint-ances, but the courier continues to be the most *intime*.[41] The young lady, however, is also very intimate with some third-rate Italians, with whom she rackets about in a way that makes much talk. Bring me that pretty novel of Cherbuliez's[42] – *Paule Méré* – and don't come later than the 23rd.'

In the natural course of events, Winterbourne, on arriving in Rome, would presently have ascertained Mrs Miller's address at the American banker's and have gone to pay his compliments to Miss Daisy. 'After what happened at Vevey I certainly think I may call upon them,' said to Mrs Costello.

'If, after what happens – at Vevey and everywhere – you desire to keep up the acquaintance, you are very welcome. Of course a man may know everyone. Men are welcome to the privilege!'

'Pray what is it that happens – here, for instance?' Winterbourne demanded.

'The girl goes about alone with her foreigners. As to

what happens further, you must apply elsewhere for information. She has picked up half a dozen of the regular Roman fortune-hunters, and she takes them about to people's houses. When she comes to a party she brings with her a gentleman with a good deal of manner and a wonderful moustache.'

'And where is the mother?'

'I haven't the least idea. They are very dreadful people.'

Winterbourne meditated a moment. 'They are very ignorant – very innocent only. Depend upon it they are not bad.'

'They are hopelessly vulgar,' said Mrs Costello. 'Whether or no being hopelessly vulgar is being "bad" is a question for the metaphysicians. They are bad enough to dislike, at any rate; and for this short life that is quite enough.'

The news that Daisy Miller was surrounded by half a dozen wonderful moustaches checked Winterbourne's impulse to go straightway to see her. He had perhaps not definitely flattered himself that he had made an ineffaceable impression upon her heart, but he was annoyed at hearing of a state of affairs so little in harmony with an image that had lately flitted in and out of his own meditations; the image of a very pretty girl looking out of an old Roman window and asking herself urgently when Mr Winterbourne would arrive. If, however, he determined to wait a little before reminding Miss Miller of his claims to her consideration, he went very soon to call upon two or three other friends. One of these friends was an American lady who had spent several winters at Geneva, where she had placed her children at school. She was a very accomplished woman and she lived in the Via Gregoriana. Winterbourne found her in a little crimson drawing-room, on a third floor; the room was filled with southern sunshine. He had not been there ten

minutes when the servant came in, announcing
'Madame Mila!' This announcement was presently followed by the entrance of little Randolph Miller, who
stopped in the middle of the room and stood staring at
Winterbourne. An instant later his pretty sister crossed
the threshold; and then, after a considerable interval,
Mrs Miller slowly advanced.

'I know you!' said Randolph.

'I'm sure you know a great many things,' exclaimed
Winterbourne, taking him by the hand. 'How is your
education coming on?'

Daisy was exchanging greetings very prettily with her
hostess; but when she heard Winterbourne's voice she
quickly turned her head. 'Well, I declare!' she said.

'I told you I should come, you know,' Winterbourne
rejoined, smiling.

'Well – I didn't believe it,' said Miss Daisy.

'I am much obliged to you,' laughed the young man.

'You might have come to see me!' said Daisy.

'I arrived only yesterday.'

'I don't believe that!' the young girl declared.

Winterbourne turned with a protesting smile to her
mother; but this lady evaded his glance, and seating herself, fixed her eyes upon her son. 'We've got a bigger
place than this,' said Randolph. 'It's all gold on the
walls.'

Mrs Miller turned uneasily in her chair. 'I told you if I
were to bring you, you would say something!' she murmured.

'I told *you!*' Randolph exclaimed. 'I tell *you*, sir!' he
added jocosely, giving Winterbourne a thump on the
knee. 'It *is* bigger, too!'

Daisy had entered upon a lively conversation with her
hostess; Winterbourne judged it becoming to address a
few words to her mother. 'I hope you have been well
since we parted at Vevey,' he said.

Mrs Miller now certainly looked at him – at his chin. 'Not very well, sir,' she answered.

'She's got the dyspepsia,'[43] said Randolph. 'I've got it too. Father's got it. I've got it worst!'

This announcement, instead of embarrassing Mrs Miller, seemed to relieve her. 'I suffer from the liver,' she said. 'I think it's this climate; it's less bracing than Schenectady, especially in the winter season. I don't know whether you know we reside at Schenectady. I was saying to Daisy that I certainly hadn't found anyone like Dr Davis, and I didn't believe I should. Oh, at Schenectady, he stands first; they think everything of him. He has so much to do, and yet there was nothing he wouldn't do for me. He said he never saw anything like my dyspepsia, but he was bound to cure it. I'm sure there was nothing he wouldn't try. He was just going to try something new when we came off. Mr Miller wanted Daisy to see Europe for herself. But I wrote to Mr Miller that it seems as if I couldn't get on without Dr Davis. At Schenectady he stands at the very top; and there's a great deal of sickness there, too. It affects my sleep.'

Winterbourne had a good deal of pathological gossip with Dr Davis's patient, during which Daisy chattered unremittingly to her own companion. The young man asked Mrs Miller how she was pleased with Rome. 'Well, I must say I am disappointed,' she answered. 'We had heard so much about it; I suppose we had heard too much. But we couldn't help that. We had been led to expect something different.'

'Ah, wait a little, and you will become very fond of it,' said Winterbourne.

'I hate it worse and worse every day!' cried Randolph.

'You are like the infant Hannibal,'[44] said Winterbourne.

'No, I ain't!' Randolph declared, at a venture.

'You are not much like an infant,' said his mother. 'But

we have seen places,' she resumed, 'that I should put a long way before Rome.' And in reply to Winterbourne's interrogation, 'There's Zürich,'[45] she observed; 'I think Zürich is lovely; and we hadn't heard half so much about it.'

'The best place we've seen is the *City of Richmond*!' said Randolph.

'He means the ship,' his mother explained. 'We crossed in that ship. Randolph had a good time on the *City of Richmond*.'

'It's the best place I've seen,' the child repeated. 'Only it was turned the wrong way.'

'Well, we've got to turn the right way some time,' said Mrs Miller, with a little laugh. Winterbourne expressed the hope that her daughter at least found some gratification in Rome, and she declared that Daisy was quite carried away. 'It's on account of the society – the society's splendid. She goes round everywhere; she has made a great number of acquaintances. Of course she goes round more than I do. I must say they have been very sociable; they have taken her right in. And then she knows a great many gentlemen. Oh, she thinks there's nothing like Rome. Of course, it's a great deal pleasanter for a young lady if she knows plenty of gentlemen.'

By this time Daisy had turned her attention again to Winterbourne. 'I've been telling Mrs Walker how mean you were!' the young girl announced.

'And what is the evidence you have offered?' asked Winterbourne, rather annoyed at Miss Miller's want of appreciation of the zeal of an admirer who on his way down to Rome had stopped neither at Bologna nor at Florence,[46] simply because of a certain sentimental impatience. He remembered that a cynical compatriot had once told him that American women – the pretty ones, and this gave a largeness to the axiom – were at once the most exacting in the world and the least endowed with a sense of indebtedness.

'Why, you were awfully mean at Vevey,' said Daisy. 'You wouldn't do anything. You wouldn't stay there when I asked you.'

'My dearest young lady,' cried Winterbourne, with eloquence, 'have I come all the way to Rome to encounter your reproaches?'

'Just hear him say that!' said Daisy to her hostess, giving a twist to a bow on this lady's dress. 'Did you ever hear anything so quaint?'[47]

'So quaint, my dear?' murmured Mrs Walker, in the tone of a partisan of Winterbourne.

'Well, I don't know,' said Daisy, fingering Mrs Walker's ribbons. 'Mrs Walker, I want to tell you something.'

'Motherr,' interposed Randolph, with his rough ends to his words, 'I tell you you've got to go. Eugenio'll raise something!'[48]

'I'm not afraid of Eugenio,' said Daisy, with a toss of her head. 'Look here, Mrs Walker,' she went on, 'you know I'm coming to your party.'

'I am delighted to hear it.'

'I've got a lovely dress.'

'I am very sure of that.'

'But I want to ask a favour – permission to bring a friend.'

'I shall be happy to see any of your friends,' said Mrs Walker, turning with a smile to Mrs Miller.

'Oh, they are not my friends,' answered Daisy's mamma, smiling shyly, in her own fashion. 'I never spoke to them!'

'It's an intimate friend of mine – Mr Giovanelli,'[49] said Daisy, without a tremor in her clear little voice or a shadow on her brilliant little face.

Mrs Walker was silent a moment, she gave a rapid

glance at Winterbourne. 'I shall be glad to see Mr Giovanelli,' she then said.

'He's an Italian,' Daisy pursued, with the prettiest ser-
enity. 'He's a great friend of mine – he's the handsomest
man in the world – except Mr Winterbourne! He knows
plenty of Italians, but he wants to know some Americans. He thinks ever so much of Americans. He's tremendously clever. He's perfectly lovely!'

It was settled that this brilliant personage should be
brought to Mrs Walker's party, and then Mrs Miller prepared to take her leave. 'I guess we'll go back to the
hotel,' she said.

'You may go back to the hotel, mother, but I'm going
to take a walk,' said Daisy.

'She's going to walk with Mr Giovanelli,' Randolph
proclaimed.

'I am going to the Pincio,' said Daisy, smiling.

'Alone, my dear – at this hour?' Mrs Walker asked. The
afternoon was drawing to a close – it was the hour for
the throng of carriages and of contemplative pedestrians.
'I don't think it's safe, my dear,' said Mrs Walker.

'Neither do I,' subjoined Mrs Miller. 'You'll get the
fever[50] as sure as you live. Remember what Dr Davis told
you!'

'Give her some medicine before she goes,' said
Randolph.

The company had risen to its feet; Daisy, still showing
her pretty teeth, bent over and kissed her hostess. 'Mrs
Walker, you are too perfect,' she said. 'I'm not going
alone; I am going to meet a friend.'

'Your friend won't keep you from getting the fever,'[51]
Mrs Miller observed.

'Is it Mr Giovanelli?' asked the hostess.

Winterbourne was watching the young girl; at this
question his attention quickened. She stood there smiling and smoothing her bonnet-ribbons; she glanced at

Winterbourne. Then, while she glanced and smiled, she answered – without a shade of hesitation, 'Mr Giovanelli – the beautiful Giovanelli.'

'My dear young friend,' said Mrs Walker, taking her hand, pleadingly, 'don't walk off to the Pincio at this hour to meet a beautiful Italian.'

'Well, he speaks English,' said Mrs Miller.

'Gracious me!' Daisy exclaimed, 'I don't want to do anything improper. There's an easy way to settle it.' She continued to glance at Winterbourne. 'The Pincio is only a hundred yards distant, and if Mr Winterbourne were as polite as he pretends he would offer to walk with me!'

Winterbourne's politeness hastened to affirm itself, and the young girl gave him gracious leave to accompany her. They passed downstairs before her mother, and at the door Winterbourne perceived Mrs Miller's carriage drawn up, with the ornamental courier whose acquaintance he had made at Vevey seated within. 'Good-bye, Eugenio!' cried Daisy, 'I'm going to take a walk.' The distance from the Via Gregoriana to the beautiful garden at the other end of the Pincian Hill is, in fact, rapidly traversed. As the day was splendid, however, and the concourse of vehicles, walkers, and loungers numerous, the young Americans found their progress much delayed. This fact was highly agreeable to Winterbourne, in spite of his consciousness of his singular situation. The slow-moving, idly gazing Roman crowd bestowed much attention upon the extremely pretty young foreign lady who was passing through it upon his arm; and he wondered what on earth had been in Daisy's mind when she proposed to expose herself, unattended, to its appreciation. His own mission, to her sense, apparently, was to consign her to the hands of Mr Giovanelli; but Winterbourne, at once annoyed and gratified, resolved that he would do no such thing.

'Why haven't you been to see me?' asked Daisy. 'You can't get out of that.'

'I have had the honour of telling you that I have only just stepped out of the train.'

'You must have stayed in the train a good while after it stopped!' cried the young girl, with her little laugh. 'I suppose you were asleep. You have had time to go to see Mrs Walker.'

'I knew Mrs Walker –' Winterbourne began to explain.

'I knew where you knew her. You knew her at Geneva. She told me so. Well, you knew me at Vevey. That's just as good. So you ought to have come.' She asked him no other question than this; she began to prattle about her own affairs. 'We've got splendid rooms at the hotel; Eugenio says they're the best rooms in Rome. We are going to stay all winter – if we don't die of the fever; and I guess we'll stay then. It's a great deal nicer than I thought; I thought it would be fearfully quiet; I was sure it would be awfully poky. I was sure we should be going round all the time with one of those dreadful old men that explain about the pictures and things. But we only had about a week of that, and now I'm enjoying myself. I know ever so many people, and they are all so charming. The society's extremely select. There are all kinds – English, and Germans, and Italians. I think I like the English best. I like their style of conversation. But there are some lovely Americans. I never saw anything so hospitable. There's something or other every day. There's not much dancing; but I must say I never thought dancing was everything. I was always fond of conversation. I guess I shall have plenty at Mrs Walker's – her rooms are so small.' When they had passed the gate of the Pincian Gardens, Miss Miller began to wonder where Mr Giovanelli might be. 'We had better go straight to that place in front,' she said, 'where you look at the view.'

'I certainly shall not help you to find him,' Winterbourne declared.

'Then I shall find him without you,' said Miss Daisy.

'You certainly won't leave me!' cried Winterbourne.

She burst into her little laugh. 'Are you afraid you'll
get lost – or run over? But there's Giovanelli, leaning
against that tree. He's staring at the women in the carriages: did you ever see anything so cool?'

Winterbourne perceived at some distance a little man
standing with folded arms, nursing his cane. He had a
handsome face, an artfully poised hat, a glass in one
eye,[52] and a nosegay in his button-hole.[53] Winterbourne
looked at him a moment and then said, 'Do you mean to
speak to that man?'

'Do I mean to speak to him? Why, you don't suppose
I mean to communicate by signs?'

'Pray understand, then,' said Winterbourne, 'that I
intend to remain with you.'

Daisy stopped and looked at him, without a sign of
troubled consciousness in her face; with nothing but the
presence of her charming eyes and her happy dimples.
'Well, she's a cool one!' thought the young man.

'I don't like the way you say that,' said Daisy. 'It's too
imperious.'

'I beg your pardon if I say it wrong. The main point is
to give you an idea of my meaning.'

The young girl looked at him more gravely, but with
eyes that were prettier than ever. 'I have never allowed a
gentleman to dictate to me, or to interfere with anything I
do.'

'I think you have made a mistake,' said Winterbourne.
'You should sometimes listen to a gentleman – the right
one.'

Daisy began to laugh again, 'I do nothing but listen to
gentlemen!' she exclaimed. 'Tell me if Mr Giovanelli is
the right one?'

The gentleman with the nosegay in his bosom had
now perceived our two friends, and was approaching
the young girl with obsequious rapidity. He bowed to
Winterbourne as well as to the latter's companion; he
had a brilliant smile, an intelligent eye; Winterbourne
thought him not a bad-looking fellow. But he nevertheless said to Daisy – 'No, he's not the right one.'

Daisy evidently had a natural talent for performing
introductions; she mentioned the name of each of her
companions to the other. She strolled along with one
of them on each side of her; Mr Giovanelli, who spoke
English very cleverly – Winterbourne afterwards learned
that he had practised the idiom upon a great many American heiresses – addressed her a great deal of very polite
nonsense; he was extremely urbane, and the young
American, who said nothing, reflected upon that pro-
fundity of Italian cleverness which enables people to
appear more gracious in proportion as they are more
acutely disappointed. Giovanelli, of course, had counted
upon something more intimate; he had not bargained for
a party of three. But he kept his temper in a manner
which suggested far-stretching intentions. Winterbourne flattered himself that he had taken his measure.
'He is not a gentleman,' said the young American; 'he is
only a clever imitation of one. He is a music-master, or
a penny-a-liner,[54] or a third-rate artist. Damn his good
looks!' Mr Giovanelli had certainly a very pretty face;
but Winterbourne felt a superior indignation at his own
lovely fellow-countrywoman's not knowing the difference between a spurious gentleman and a real one. Giovanelli chattered and jested and made himself
wonderfully agreeable. It was true that if he was an imitation the imitation was very skilful. 'Nevertheless,'
Winterbourne said to himself, 'a nice girl ought to know!'
And then he came back to the question whether this was
in fact a nice girl. Would a nice girl – even allowing for

her being a little American flirt – make a rendezvous with a presumably low-lived foreigner?[55] The rendezvous in this case, indeed, had been in broad daylight, and in the most crowded corner of Rome; but was it not impossible to regard the choice of these circumstances as a proof of extreme cynicism? Singular though it may seem, Winterbourne was vexed that the young girl, in joining her *amoroso*,[56] should not appear more impatient of his own company, and he was vexed because of his inclination. It was impossible to regard her as a perfectly well-conducted young lady; she was wanting in a certain indispensable delicacy. It would therefore simplify matters greatly to be able to treat her as the object of one of those sentiments which are called by romancers 'lawless passions'. That she should seem to wish to get rid of him would help him to think more lightly of her, and to be able to think more lightly of her would make her much less perplexing. But Daisy, on this occasion, continued to present herself as an inscrutable combination of audacity and innocence.

She had been walking some quarter of an hour, attended by her two cavaliers, and responding in a tone of very childish gaiety, as it seemed to Winterbourne, to the pretty speeches of Mr Giovanelli, when a carriage that had detached itself from the revolving train[57] drew up beside the path. At the same moment Winterbourne perceived that his friend Mrs Walker – the lady whose house he had lately left – was seated in the vehicle and was beckoning to him. Leaving Miss Miller's side, he hastened to obey her summons. Mrs Walker was flushed; she wore an excited air. 'It is really too dreadful,' she said. 'That girl must not do this sort of thing. She must not walk here with you two men. Fifty people have noticed her.'

Winterbourne raised his eyebrows. 'I think it's a pity to make too much fuss about it.'

'It's a pity to let the girl ruin herself!'

'She is very innocent,' said Winterbourne.

'She's very crazy!' cried Mrs Walker. 'Did you ever see anything so imbecile as her mother? After you had all left me, just now, I could not sit still for thinking of it. It seemed too pitiful, not even to attempt to save her. I ordered the carriage and put on my bonnet, and came here as quickly as possible. Thank heaven I have found you!'

'What do you propose to do with us?' asked Winterbourne, smiling.

'To ask her to get in, to drive her about here for half an hour, so that the world may see she is not running absolutely wild, and then to take her safely home.'

'I don't think it's a very happy thought,' said Winterbourne; 'but you can try.'

Mrs Walker tried. The young man went in pursuit of Miss Miller, who had simply nodded and smiled at his interlocutrix in the carriage and had gone her way with her own companion. Daisy, on learning that Mrs Walker wished to speak to her, retraced her steps with a perfect good grace and with Mr Giovanelli at her side. She declared that she was delighted to have a chance to present this gentleman to Mrs Walker. She immediately achieved the introduction, and declared that she had never in her life seen anything so lovely as Mrs Walker's carriage-rug.

'I am glad you admire it,' said this lady, smiling sweetly. 'Will you get in and let me put it over you?'

'Oh, no, thank you,' said Daisy. 'I shall admire it much more as I see you driving round with it.'

'Do get in and drive with me,' said Mrs Walker.

'That would be charming, but it's so enchanting just as I am!' and Daisy gave a brilliant glance at the gentlemen on either side of her.

'It may be enchanting, dear child, but it is not the

custom here,' urged Mrs Walker, leaning forward in her victoria[58] with her hands devoutly clasped.

'Well, it ought to be, then!' said Daisy. 'If I didn't walk I should expire.'

'You should walk with your mother, dear,' cried the lady from Geneva, losing patience.

'With my mother dear!' exclaimed the young girl. Winterbourne saw that she scented interference. 'My mother never walked ten steps in her life. And then, you know,' she added with a laugh, 'I am more than five years old.'

'You are old enough to be more reasonable. You are old enough, dear Miss Miller, to be talked about.'

Daisy looked at Mrs Walker, smiling intensely. 'Talked about? What do you mean!'

'Come into my carriage and I will tell you.'

Daisy turned her quickened glance again from one of the gentlemen beside her to the other. Mr Giovanelli was bowing to and fro, rubbing down his gloves and laughing very agreeably; Winterbourne thought it a most unpleasant scene. 'I don't think I want to know what you mean,' said Daisy presently. 'I don't think I should like it.'

Winterbourne wished that Mrs Walker would tuck in her carriage-rug and drive away; but this lady did not enjoy being defied, as she afterwards told him. 'Should you prefer being thought a very reckless girl?' she demanded.

'Gracious me!' exclaimed Daisy. She looked again at Mr Giovanelli, then she turned to Winterbourne. There was a little pink flush in her cheek; she was tremendously pretty. 'Does Mr Winterbourne think,' she asked slowly, smiling, throwing back her head and glancing at him from head to foot, 'that – to save my reputation – I ought to get into the carriage?'

Winterbourne coloured; for an instant he hesitated

greatly. It seemed so strange to hear her speak that way of her 'reputation'. But he himself, in fact, must speak in accordance with gallantry. The finest gallantry, here, was simply to tell her the truth; and the truth, for Winterbourne, as the few indications I have been able to give have made him known to the reader, was that Daisy Miller should take Mrs Walker's advice. He looked at her exquisite prettiness; and then he said very gently, 'I think you should get into the carriage.'

Daisy gave a violent laugh. 'I never heard anything so stiff! If this is improper, Mrs Walker,' she pursued, 'then I am all improper, and you must give me up. Good-bye; I hope you'll have a lovely ride!' and, with Mr Giovanelli, who made a triumphantly obsequious salute, she turned away.

Mrs Walker sat looking after her, and there were tears in Mrs Walker's eyes. 'Get in here, sir,' she said to Winterbourne, indicating the place beside her. The young man answered that he felt bound to accompany Miss Miller; whereupon Mrs Walker declared that if he refused her this favour she would never speak to him again. She was evidently in earnest. Winterbourne overtook Daisy and her companion and, offering the young girl his hand, told her that Mrs Walker had made an imperious claim upon his society. He expected that in answer she would say something rather free, something to commit herself still further to that 'recklessness' from which Mrs Walker had so charitably endeavoured to dissuade her. But she only shook his hand, hardly looking at him, while Mr Giovanelli bade him farewell with a too emphatic flourish of the hat.

Winterbourne was not in the best possible humour as he took his seat in Mrs Walker's victoria. 'That was not clever of you,' he said candidly, while the vehicle mingled again with the throng of carriages.

'In such a case,' his companion answered, 'I don't wish to be clever, I wish to be *earnest*!'

'Well, your earnestness has only offended her and put her off.'

'It has happened very well,' said Mrs Walker. 'If she is so perfectly determined to compromise herself, the sooner one knows it the better; one can act accordingly.'

'I suspect she meant no harm,' Winterbourne rejoined.

'So I thought a month ago. But she has been going too far.'

'What has she been doing?'

'Everything that is not done here. Flirting with any man she could pick up; sitting in corners with mysterious Italians; dancing all the evening with the same partners; receiving visits at eleven o'clock at night. Her mother goes away when visitors come.'

'But her brother,' said Winterbourne, laughing, 'sits up till midnight.'

'He must be edified by what he sees. I'm told that at their hotel everyone is talking about her, and that a smile goes round among the servants when a gentleman comes and asks for Miss Miller.'

'The servants be hanged!' said Winterbourne angrily. 'The poor girl's only fault,' he presently added, 'is that she is very uncultivated.'

'She is naturally indelicate,' Mrs Walker declared. 'Take that example this morning. How long had you known her at Vevey?'

'A couple of days.'

'Fancy, then, her making it a personal matter that you should have left the place!'

Winterbourne was silent for some moments; then he said 'I suspect, Mrs Walker, that you and I have lived too long at Geneva!' And he added a request that she should inform him with what particular design she had made him enter her carriage.

'I wished to beg you to cease your relations with Miss
Miller – not to flirt with her – to give her no further opportunity to expose herself – to let her alone, in short.'

'I'm afraid I can't do that,' said Winterbourne. 'I like
her extremely.'

'All the more reason that you shouldn't help her to
make a scandal.'

'There shall be nothing scandalous in my attentions to
her.'

'There certainly will be in the way she takes them. But
I have said what I had on my conscience,' Mrs Walker
pursued. 'If you wish to rejoin the young lady I will put
you down. Here, by the way, you have a chance.'

The carriage was traversing that part of the Pincian
Garden which overhangs the wall of Rome and overlooks
the beautiful Villa Borghese. It is bordered by a large
parapet, near which there are several seats. One of the
seats, at a distance, was occupied by a gentleman and a
lady, towards whom Mrs Walker gave a toss of her head.
At the same moment these persons rose and walked
towards the parapet. Winterbourne had asked the coach-
man to stop; he now descended from the carriage. His
companion looked at him a moment in silence; then,
while he raised his hat, she drove majestically away.
Winterbourne stood there; he had turned his eyes
towards Daisy and her cavalier. They evidently saw no
one; they were too deeply occupied with each other.
When they reached the low garden-wall they stood a
moment looking off at the great flat-topped pine-clusters
of the Villa Borghese; then Giovanelli seated himself
familiarly upon the broad ledge of the wall. The western
sun in the opposite sky sent out a brilliant shaft through
a couple of cloud-bars; whereupon Daisy's companion
took her parasol out of her hands and opened it. She
came a little nearer and he held the parasol over her;
then, still holding it, he let it rest upon her shoulder, so

Daisy Miller

that both their heads were hidden from Winterbourne. This young man lingered a moment, then he began to walk. But he walked – not towards the couple with the parasol; towards the residence of his aunt, Mrs Costello.

4

He flattered himself on the following day that there was no smiling among the servants when he, at least, asked for Mrs Miller at her hotel. This lady and her daughter, however, were not at home; and on the next day, after repeating his visit, Winterbourne again had the misfortune not to find them. Mrs Walker's party took place on the evening of the third day, and in spite of the frigidity of his last interview with the hostess, Winterbourne was among the guests. Mrs Walker was one of those American ladies who, while residing abroad, make a point, in their own phrase, of studying European society; and she had on this occasion collected several specimens of her diversely born fellow-mortals to serve, as it were, as text-books. When Winterbourne arrived Daisy Miller was not there; but in a few moments he saw her mother come in alone, very shyly and ruefully. Mrs Miller's hair, above her exposed-looking temples, was more frizzled than ever. As she approached Mrs Walker, Winterbourne also drew near.

'You see I've come all alone,' said poor Mrs Miller. 'I'm so frightened; I don't know what to do; it's the first time I've ever been to a party alone – especially in this country. I wanted to bring Randolph or Eugenio, or someone, but Daisy just pushed me off by myself. I ain't used to going round alone.'

'And does not your daughter intend to favour us with her society?' demanded Mrs Walker, impressively.

'Well, Daisy's all dressed,' said Mrs Miller, with that accent of the dispassionate, if not the philosophic, historian with which she always recorded the current incidents of her daughter's career. 'She's got dressed on purpose before dinner. But she's got a friend of hers there; that gentleman – the Italian – that she wanted to bring. They've got going at the piano; it seems as if they couldn't leave off. Mr Giovanelli sings splendidly. But I guess they'll come before very long,' concluded Mrs Miller hopefully.

'I'm sorry she should come – in that way,' said Mrs Walker.

'Well, I told her that there was no use in her getting dressed before dinner if she was going to wait three hours,' responded Daisy's mamma. 'I didn't see the use of her putting on such a dress as that to sit round with Mr Giovanelli.'

'This is most horrible!' said Mrs Walker, turning away and addressing herself to Winterbourne. '*Elle s'affiche*.[59] It's her revenge for my having ventured to remonstrate with her. When she comes I shall not speak to her.'

Daisy came after eleven o'clock, but she was not, on such an occasion, a young lady to wait to be spoken to. She rustled forward in radiant loveliness, smiling and chattering, carrying a large bouquet and attended by Mr Giovanelli. Everyone stopped talking and turned and looked at her. She came straight to Mrs Walker. 'I'm afraid you thought I never was coming, so I sent mother off to tell you. I wanted to make Mr Giovanelli practise some things before he came; you know he sings beautifully, and I want you to ask him to sing. This is Mr Giovanelli; you know I introduced him to you; he's got the most lovely voice and he knows the most charming set

of songs. I made him go over them this evening, on purpose; we had the greatest time at the hotel.' Of all this
Daisy delivered herself with the sweetest, brightest aud-
ibleness, looking now at her hostess and now round the
room, while she gave a series of little pats, round her
shoulders, to the edges of her dress. 'Is there anyone I
know?' she asked.

'I think everyone knows you!' said Mrs Walker preg-
nantly, and she gave a very cursory greeting to Mr Giovanelli. This gentleman bore himself gallantly. He smiled
and bowed and showed his white teeth, he curled his
moustaches and rolled his eyes, and performed all the
proper functions of a handsome Italian at an evening
party. He sang, very prettily, half a dozen songs, though
Mrs Walker afterwards declared that she had been quite
unable to find out who asked him. It was apparently
not Daisy who had given him his orders. Daisy sat at a
distance from the piano, and though she had publicly,
as it were, professed a high admiration for his singing,
talked, not inaudibly, while it was going on.

'It's a pity these rooms are so small; we can't dance,'
she said to Winterbourne, as if she had seen him five
minutes before.

'I am not sorry we can't dance,' Winterbourne
answered; 'I don't dance.'

'Of course you don't dance; you're too stiff,' said Miss
Daisy. 'I hope you enjoyed your drive with Mrs Walker.'

'No I didn't enjoy it; I preferred walking with you.'

'We paired off, that was much better,' said Daisy. 'But
did you ever hear anything so cool as Mrs Walker's wanting me to get into her carriage and drop poor Mr Giovanelli; and under the pretext that it was proper? People
have different ideas! It would have been most unkind;
he had been talking about that walk for ten days.'

'He should not have talked about it at all,' said Winterbourne; 'he would never have proposed to a young

lady of this country to walk about the streets with him.'

'About the streets?' cried Daisy, with her pretty stare. 'Where then would he have proposed to her to walk? The Pincio is not the streets, either; and I, thank goodness, am not a young lady of this country. The young ladies of this country have a dreadfully poky time of it, so far as I can learn; I don't see why I should change my habits for *them.*'

'I am afraid your habits are those of a flirt,' said Winterbourne gravely.

'Of course they are,' she cried, giving him her little smiling stare again. 'I'm a fearful, frightful flirt! Did you ever hear of a nice girl that was not? But I suppose you will tell me now that I am not a nice girl.'

'You're a very nice girl, but I wish you would flirt with me, and me only,' said Winterbourne.

'Ah! thank you, thank you very much; you are the last man I should think of flirting with. As I have had the pleasure of informing you, you are too stiff.'

'You say that too often,' said Winterbourne.

Daisy gave a delighted laugh. 'If I could have the sweet hope of making you angry, I would say it again.'

'Don't do that; when I am angry I'm stiffer than ever. But if you won't flirt with me, do cease at least to flirt with your friend at the piano; they don't understand that sort of thing here.'

'I thought they understood nothing else!' exclaimed Daisy.

'Not in young unmarried women.'

'It seems to me much more proper in young unmarried women than in old married ones,'[60] Daisy declared.

'Well,' said Winterbourne, 'when you deal with natives you must go by the custom of the place. Flirting is a purely American custom; it doesn't exist here. So when you show yourself in public with Mr Giovanelli and without your mother –'

'Gracious! Poor mother!' interposed Daisy.

'Though you may be flirting, Mr Giovanelli is not; he means something else.'

'He isn't preaching, at any rate,' said Daisy with vivacity. 'And if you want very much to know, we are neither of us flirting; we are too good friends for that; we are very intimate friends.'

'Ah,' rejoined Winterbourne, 'if you are in love with each other it is another affair.'

She had allowed him up to this point to talk so frankly that he had no expectation of shocking her by this ejaculation; but she immediately got up, blushing visibly, and leaving him to exclaim mentally that little American flirts were the queerest creatures in the world. 'Mr Giovanelli, at least,' she said, giving her interlocutor a single glance, 'never says such very disagreeable things to me.'

Winterbourne was bewildered; he stood staring. Mr Giovanelli had finished singing; he left the piano and came over to Daisy. 'Won't you come into the other room and have some tea?' he asked, bending before her with his decorative smile.

Daisy turned to Winterbourne, beginning to smile again. He was still more perplexed, for this inconsequent smile made nothing clear, though it seemed to prove, indeed, that she had a sweetness and softness that reverted instinctively to the pardon of offences. 'It has never occurred to Mr Winterbourne to offer me any tea,' she said, with her little tormenting manner.

'I have offered you advice,' Winterbourne rejoined.

'I prefer weak tea!' cried Daisy, and she went off with the brilliant Giovanelli. She sat with him in the adjoining room, in the embrasure of the window, for the rest of the evening. There was an interesting performance at the piano, but neither of these young people gave heed to it. When Daisy came to take leave of Mrs Walker, this lady conscientiously repaired the weakness of which she had

been guilty at the moment of the young girl's arrival. She
turned her back straight upon Miss Miller and left her to
depart with what grace she might. Winterbourne was
standing near the door; he saw it all. Daisy turned very
pale and looked at her mother, but Mrs Miller was hum-
bly unconscious of any violation of the usual social
forms. She appeared, indeed, to have felt an incongruous impulse to draw attention to her own striking observ-
ance of them. 'Goodnight, Mrs Walker,' she said; 'we've
had a beautiful evening. You see if I let Daisy come to
parties without me, I don't want her to go away without
me.' Daisy turned away, looking with a pale, grave face
at the circle near the door; Winterbourne saw that, for
the first moment, she was too much shocked and puzzled even for indignation. He on his side was greatly
touched.

'That was very cruel,' he said to Mrs Walker.

'She never enters my drawing-room again,' replied his
hostess.

Since Winterbourne was not to meet her in Mrs
Walker's drawing-room, he went as often as possible to
Mrs Miller's hotel. The ladies were rarely at home, but
when he found them the devoted Giovanelli was always
present. Very often the polished little Roman was in the
drawing-room with Daisy alone, Mrs Miller being apparently constantly of the opinion that discretion is the
better part of surveillance. Winterbourne noted, at first
with surprise, that Daisy on these occasions was never
embarrassed or annoyed by his own entrance; but he
very presently began to feel that she had no more sur-
prises for him; the unexpected in her behaviour was the
only thing to expect. She showed no displeasure at her
tête-à-tête with Giovanelli being interrupted; she could
chatter as freshly and freely with two gentlemen as with
one; there was always, in her conversation, the same odd
mixture of audacity and puerility. Winterbourne

remarked to himself that if she was seriously interested in Giovanelli it was very singular that she should not take more trouble to preserve the sanctity of their interviews, and he liked her the more for her innocent-looking indifference and her apparently inexhaustible good humour. He could hardly have said why, but she seemed to him a girl who would never be jealous. At the risk of exciting a somewhat derisive smile on the reader's part, I may affirm that with regard to the women who had hitherto interested him it very often seemed to Winterbourne among the possibilities that, given certain contingencies, he should be afraid – literally afraid – of these ladies. He had a pleasant sense that he should never be afraid of Daisy Miller. It must be added that this sentiment was not altogether flattering to Daisy; it was part of his conviction, or rather of his apprehension, that she would prove a very light young person.

But she was evidently very much interested in Giovanelli. She looked at him whenever he spoke; she was perpetually telling him to do this and to do that; she was constantly 'chaffing' and abusing him. She appeared completely to have forgotten that Winterbourne had said anything to displease her at Mrs Walker's little party. One Sunday afternoon, having gone to St Peter's with his aunt, Winterbourne perceived Daisy strolling about the great church in company with the inevitable Giovanelli. Presently he pointed out the young girl and her cavalier to Mrs Costello. This lady looked at them a moment through her eyeglass, and then she said:

'That's what makes you so pensive in these days, eh?'

'I had not the least idea I was pensive,' said the young man.

'You are very much preoccupied, you are thinking of something.'

'And what is it,' he asked, 'that you accuse me of thinking of?'

'Of that young lady's, Miss Baker's, Miss Chandler's[61] – what's her name? – Miss Miller's intrigue[62] with that little barber's block.'[63]

'Do you call it an intrigue,' Winterbourne asked – 'an affair that goes on with such peculiar publicity?'

'That's their folly,' said Mrs Costello, 'it's not their merit.'

'No,' rejoined Winterbourne, with something of that pensiveness to which his aunt had alluded. 'I don't believe that there is anything to be called an intrigue.'

'I have heard a dozen people speak of it; they say she is quite carried away by him.'

'They are certainly very intimate,' said Winterbourne.

Mrs Costello inspected the young couple again with her optical instrument. 'He is very handsome. One easily sees how it is. She thinks him the most elegant man in the world, the finest gentleman. She has never seen anything like him; he is better even than the courier. It was the courier probably who introduced him, and if he succeeds in marrying the young lady, the courier will come in for a magnificent commission.'

'I don't believe she thinks of marrying him,' said Winterbourne, 'and I don't believe he hopes to marry her.'

'You may be very sure she thinks of nothing. She goes on from day to day, from hour to hour, as they did in the Golden Age.[64] I can imagine nothing more vulgar. And at the same time,' added Mrs Costello, 'depend upon it that she may tell you any moment that she is "engaged".'

'I think that is more than Giovanelli expects,' said Winterbourne.

'Who is Giovanelli?'

'The little Italian. I have asked questions about him and learned something. He is apparently a perfectly respectable little man. I believe he is in a small way a *cavaliere avvocato*.[65] But he doesn't move in what are

called the first circles. I think it is really not absolutely
impossible that the courier introduced him. He is evidently immensely charmed with Miss Miller. If she
thinks him the finest gentleman in the world, he, on his
side, has never found himself in personal contact with
such splendour, such opulence, such expensiveness, as
this young lady's. And then she must seem to him wonderfully pretty and interesting. I rather doubt whether
he dreams of marrying her. That must appear to him
too impossible a piece of luck. He has nothing but his
handsome face to offer, and there is a substantial Mr
Miller in that mysterious land of dollars. Giovanelli
knows that he hasn't a title to offer. If he were only a
count or a *marchese*![66] He must wonder at his luck at the
way they have taken him up.'

'He accounts for it by his handsome face, and thinks
Miss Miller a young lady *qui se passe ses fantaisies*!'[67] said
Mrs Costello.

'It is very true,' Winterbourne pursued, 'that Daisy
and her mamma have not yet risen to that stage of – what
shall I call it? – of culture, at which the idea of catching a
count or a *marchese* begins. I believe that they are intellectually incapable of that conception.'

'Ah! but the *cavaliere* can't believe it,' said Mrs Costello.

Of the observation excited by Daisy's 'intrigue',
Winterbourne gathered that day at St Peter's sufficient
evidence. A dozen of the American colonists in Rome
came to talk with Mrs Costello, who sat on a little portable stool at the base of one of the great pilasters. The
vesper-service[68] was going forward in splendid chants
and organ-tones in the adjacent choir, and meanwhile,
between Mrs Costello and her friends, there was a great
deal said about poor little Miss Miller's going really 'too
far'. Winterbourne was not pleased with what he heard;
but when, coming out upon the great steps of the church,
he saw Daisy, who had emerged before him, get into an
open cab with her accomplice and roll away through the

cynical streets of Rome, he could not deny to himself that she was going very far indeed. He felt very sorry for her – not exactly that he believed that she had completely lost her head, but because it was painful to hear so much that was pretty and undefended and natural assigned to a vulgar place among the categories of disorder. He made an attempt after this to give a hint to Mrs Miller. He met one day in the Corso a friend – a tourist like himself – who had just come out of the Doria Palace, where he had been walking through the beautiful gallery. His friend talked for a moment about the superb portrait of Innocent X by Velazquez,[69] which hangs in one of the cabinets of the palace, and then said, 'And in the same cabinet, by the way, I had the pleasure of contemplating a picture of a different kind – that pretty American girl whom you pointed out to me last week.' In answer to Winterbourne's inquiries, his friend narrated that the pretty American girl – prettier than ever – was seated with a companion in the secluded nook in which the great papal portrait is enshrined.

'Who was her companion?' asked Winterbourne.

'A little Italian with a bouquet in his buttonhole. The girl is delightfully pretty, but I thought I understood from you the other day that she was a young lady *du meilleur monde*.'[70]

'So she is!' answered Winterbourne; and having assured himself that his informant had seen Daisy and her companion but five minutes before, he jumped into a cab and went to call on Mrs Miller. She was at home; but she apologized to him for receiving him in Daisy's absence.

'She's gone out somewhere with Mr Giovanelli,' said Mrs Miller. 'She's always going round with Mr Giovanelli.'

'I have noticed that they are very intimate,' Winterbourne observed.

'Oh! it seems as if they couldn't live without each

other!' said Mrs Miller. 'Well, he's a real gentleman,
anyhow. I keep telling Daisy she's engaged!'

'And what does Daisy say?'

'Oh, she says she isn't engaged. But she might as well
be!' this impartial parent resumed. 'She goes on as if she
was. But I've made Mr Giovanelli promise to tell me, if
she doesn't. I should want to write to Mr Miller about it –
shouldn't you?'

Winterbourne replied that he certainly should; and the
state of mind of Daisy's mamma struck him as so unpre-
cedented in the annals of parental vigilance that he gave
up as utterly irrelevant the attempt to place her upon her
guard.

After this Daisy was never at home, and Winterbourne
ceased to meet her at the houses of their common
acquaintances, because, as he perceived, these shrewd
people had quite made up their minds that she was going
too far. They ceased to invite her, and they intimated
that they desired to express to observant Europeans the
great truth that, though Miss Daisy Miller was a young
American lady, her behaviour was not representative –
was regarded by her compatriots as abnormal. Winterbourne wondered how she felt about all the cold shoulders that were turned towards her, and sometimes it
annoyed him to suspect that she did not feel at all. He
said to himself that she was too light and childish, too
uncultivated and unreasoning, too provincial, to have
reflected upon her ostracism or even to have perceived
it. Then at other moments he believed that she carried
about in her elegant and irresponsible little organism a
defiant, passionate, perfectly observant consciousness of
the impression she produced. He asked himself whether
Daisy's defiance came from the consciousness of innocence or from her being, essentially, a young person of the
reckless class. It must be admitted that holding oneself to

a belief in Daisy's 'innocence' came to seem to Winterbourne more and more a matter of fine-spun gallantry. As I have already had occasion to relate, he was angry at finding himself reduced to chopping logic about this young lady; he was vexed at his want of instinctive certitude as to how far her eccentricities were generic, national, and how far they were personal. From either view of them he had somehow missed her, and now it was too late. She was 'carried away' by Mr Giovanelli.

A few days after his brief interview with her mother, he encountered her in that beautiful abode of flowering desolation known as the Palace of the Caesars. The early Roman spring had filled the air with bloom and perfume, and the rugged surface of the Palatine was muffled with tender verdure. Daisy was strolling along the top of one of those great mounds of ruin that are embanked with mossy marble and paved with monumental inscriptions. It seemed to him that Rome had never been so lovely as just then. He stood looking off at the enchanting harmony of line and colour that remotely encircles the city, inhaling the softly humid odours and feeling the freshness of the year and the antiquity of the place reaffirm themselves in mysterious interfusion. It seemed to him also that Daisy had never looked so pretty; but this had been an observation of his whenever he met her. Giovanelli was at her side, and Giovanelli, too, wore an aspect of even unwonted brilliancy.

'Well,' said Daisy, 'I should think you would be lonesome!'

'Lonesome?' asked Winterbourne.

'You are always going round by yourself. Can't you get anyone to walk with you?'

'I am not so fortunate,' said Winterbourne, 'as your companion.'

Giovanelli, from the first, had treated Winterbourne

with distinguished politeness; he listened with a deferential air to his remarks; he laughed, punctiliously, at his pleasantries; he seemed disposed to testify to his belief that Winterbourne was a superior young man. He carried himself in no degree like a jealous wooer; he had obviously a great deal of tact; he had no objection to your expecting a little humility of him. It even seemed to Winterbourne at times that Giovanelli would find a certain mental relief in being able to have a private understanding with him – to say to him, as an intelligent man, that, bless you, *he* knew how extraordinary was this young lady, and didn't flatter himself with delusive – or at least *too* delusive – hopes of matrimony and dollars. On this occasion he strolled away from his companion to pluck a sprig of almond blossom, which he carefully arranged in his button-hole.

'I know why you say that,' said Daisy, watching Giovanelli. 'Because you think I go round too much with *him*!' And she nodded at her attendant.

'Everyone thinks so – if you care to know,' said Winterbourne.

'Of course I care to know!' Daisy exclaimed seriously. 'But I don't believe it. They are only pretending to be shocked. They don't really care a straw what I do. Besides, I don't go round so much.'

'I think you will find they do care. They will show it – disagreeably.'

Daisy looked at him a moment. 'How – disagreeably?'

'Haven't you noticed anything?' Winterbourne asked.

'I have noticed you. But I noticed you were as stiff as an umbrella the first time I saw you.'

'You will find I am not so stiff as several others,' said Winterbourne, smiling.

'How shall I find it?'

'By going to see the others.'

'What will they do to me?'

'They will give you the cold shoulder. Do you know what that means?'

Daisy was looking at him intently; she began to colour. 'Do you mean as Mrs Walker did the other night?'

'Exactly!' said Winterbourne.

She looked away at Giovanelli, who was decorating himself with his almond blossom. Then looking back at Winterbourne – 'I shouldn't think you would let people be so unkind!' she said.

'How can I help it?' he asked.

'I should think you would say something.'

'I do say something'; and he paused a moment. 'I say that your mother tells me that she believes you are engaged.'

'Well, she does,' said Daisy very simply.

Winterbourne began to laugh. 'And does Randolph believe it?' he asked.

'I guess Randolph doesn't believe anything,' said Daisy. Randolph's scepticism excited Winterbourne to further hilarity, and he observed that Giovanelli was coming back to them. Daisy, observing it too, addressed herself to her countryman. 'Since you have mentioned it,' she said, 'I *am* engaged.'… Winterbourne looked at her; he had stopped laughing. 'You don't believe it!' she added.

He was silent a moment; and then, 'Yes, I believe it!' he said.

'Oh, no, you don't,' she answered. 'Well, then – I am not!'

The young girl and her cicerone[71] were on their way to the gate of the enclosure, so that Winterbourne, who had but lately entered, presently took leave of them. A week afterwards he went to dine at a beautiful villa on the Caelian Hill, and, on arriving, dismissed his hired vehicle. The evening was charming, and he promised himself the satisfaction of walking home beneath the

Arch of Constantine and past the vaguely lighted monuments of the Forum. There was a waning moon in the
sky, and her radiance was not brilliant, but she was
veiled in a thin cloud-curtain which seemed to diffuse
and equalize it. When, on his return from the villa (it was
eleven o'clock), Winterbourne approached the dusky circle of the Colosseum,[72] it occurred to him, as a lover of
the picturesque, that the interior, in the pale moonshine,
would be well worth a glance. He turned aside and
walked to one of the empty arches, near which, as he
observed, an open carriage – one of the little Roman
street-cabs – was stationed. Then he passed in among the
cavernous shadows of the great structure, and emerged
upon the clear and silent arena. The place had never
seemed to him more impressive. One half of the gigantic
circus was in deep shade; the other was sleeping in the
luminous dusk. As he stood there he began to murmur
Byron's famous lines,[73] out of *Manfred*; but before he had
finished his quotation he remembered that if nocturnal
meditations in the Colosseum are recommended by the
poets, they are deprecated by the doctors.[74] The historic
atmosphere was there, certainly; but the historic atmosphere, scientifically considered, was no better than a
villainous miasma. Winterbourne walked to the middle
of the arena, to take a more general glance, intending
thereafter to make a hasty retreat. The great cross in the
centre[75] was covered with shadow; it was only as he drew
near it that he made it out distinctly. Then he saw that
two persons were stationed upon the low steps which
formed its base. One of these was a woman, seated; her
companion was standing in front of her.

Presently the sound of the woman's voice came to him
distinctly in the warm night air. 'Well, he looks at us as
one of the old lions or tigers may have looked at the
Christian martyrs!' These were the words he heard, in
the familiar accent of Miss Daisy Miller.

'Let us hope he is not very hungry,' responded the ingenious Giovanelli. 'He will have to take me first; you will serve for dessert!'

Winterbourne stopped, with a sort of horror; and, it must be added, with a sort of relief. It was as if a sudden illumination had been flashed upon the ambiguity of Daisy's behaviour and the riddle had become easy to read. She was a young lady whom a gentleman need no longer be at pains to respect. He stood there looking at her – looking at her companion, and not reflecting that though he saw them vaguely, he himself must have been more brightly visible. He felt angry with himself that he had bothered so much about the right way of regarding Miss Daisy Miller. Then, as he was going to advance again, he checked himself; not from the fear that he was doing her injustice, but from a sense of the danger of appearing unbecomingly exhilarated by this sudden revulsion from cautious criticism. He turned away towards the entrance of the place; but as he did so he heard Daisy speak again.

'Why, it was Mr Winterbourne! He saw me – and he cuts me!'[76]

What a clever little reprobate she was, and how smartly she played an injured innocence! But he wouldn't cut her. Winterbourne came forward again, and went towards the great cross. Daisy had got up; Giovanelli lifted his hat. Winterbourne had now begun to think simply of the craziness, from a sanitary point of view, of a delicate young girl lounging away the evening in this nest of malaria. What if she *were* a clever little reprobate? That was no reason for her dying of the *perniciosa*.[77] 'How long have you been here?' he asked, almost brutally.

Daisy, lovely in the flattering moonlight, looked at him a moment. Then – 'All the evening,' she answered gently . . . 'I never saw anything so pretty.'

'I am afraid,' said Winterbourne, 'that you will not

think Roman fever very pretty. This is the way people catch it. I wonder,' he added, turning to Giovanelli, 'that you, a native Roman, should countenance such a terrible indiscretion.'

'Ah,' said the handsome native, 'for myself, I am not afraid.'

'Neither am I – for you! I am speaking for this young lady.'

Giovanelli lifted his well-shaped eyebrows and showed his brilliant teeth. But he took Winterbourne's rebuke with docility. 'I told the Signorina it was a grave indiscretion; but when was the Signorina ever prudent?'

'I never was sick, and I don't mean to be!' the Signorina declared. 'I don't look like much, but I'm healthy! I was bound to see the Colosseum by moonlight; I shouldn't have wanted to go home without that; and we have had the most beautiful time, haven't we, Mr Giovanelli! If there has been any danger, Eugenio can give me some pills. He has got some splendid pills.'[78]

'I should advise you,' said Winterbourne, 'to drive home as fast as possible and take one!'

'What you say is very wise,' Giovanelli rejoined. 'I will go and make sure the carriage is at hand.' And he went forward rapidly.

Daisy followed with Winterbourne. He kept looking at her; she seemed not in the least embarrassed. Winterbourne said nothing; Daisy chattered about the beauty of the place. 'Well, I *have* seen the Colosseum by moonlight!' she exclaimed. 'That's one good thing.'[79] Then, noticing Winterbourne's silence, she asked him why he didn't speak. He made no answer; he only began to laugh. They passed under one of the dark archways; Giovanelli was in front with the carriage. Here Daisy stopped a moment, looking at the young American. '*Did* you believe I was engaged the other day?' she asked.

'It doesn't matter what I believed the other day,' said Winterbourne, still laughing.

'Well, what do you believe now?'

'I believe that it makes very little difference whether you are engaged or not!'

He felt the young girl's pretty eyes fixed upon him through the thick gloom of the archway; she was apparently going to answer. But Giovanelli hurried her forward. 'Quick, quick,' he said; 'if we get in by midnight we are quite safe.'[80]

Daisy took her seat in the carriage, and the fortunate Italian placed himself beside her. 'Don't forget Eugenio's pills!' said Winterbourne, as he lifted his hat.

'I don't care,' said Daisy, in a little strange tone, 'whether I have Roman fever or not!'[81] Upon this the cab-driver cracked his whip, and they rolled away over the desultory[82] patches of the antique pavement.

Winterbourne – to do him justice, as it were – mentioned to no one that he had encountered Miss Miller, at midnight, in the Colosseum with a gentleman; but nevertheless, a couple of days later, the fact of her having been there under these circumstances was known to every member of the little American circle, and commented accordingly. Winterbourne reflected that they of course known it at the hotel, and that, after Daisy's return, there had been an exchange of jokes between the porter and the cab-driver. But the young man was conscious at the same moment that it had ceased to be a matter of serious regret to him that the little American flirt should be 'talked about' by low-minded menials. These people, a day or two later, had serious information to give: the little American flirt was alarmingly ill. Winterbourne, when the rumour came to him, immediately went to the hotel for more news. He found that two or three charitable friends had preceded him and that they were being entertained in Mrs Miller's salon by Randolph.

'It's going round at night,' said Randolph – 'that's what made her sick. She's always going round at night. I shouldn't think she'd want to – it's so plaguey dark. You can't see anything here at night, except when there's a moon. In America there's always a moon!' Mrs Miller was invisible; she was now, at least, giving her daughter the advantage of her society. It was evident that Daisy was dangerously ill.

Winterbourne went often to ask for news of her, and once he saw Mrs Miller, who, though deeply alarmed, was – rather to his surprise – perfectly composed, and, as it appeared, a most efficient and judicious nurse. She talked a good deal about Dr Davis, but Winterbourne paid her the compliment of saying to himself that she was not, after all, such a monstrous goose. 'Daisy spoke of you the other day,' she said to him. 'Half the time she doesn't know what she's saying, but that time I think she did. She gave me a message; she told me to tell you. She told me to tell you that she never was engaged to that handsome Italian. I am sure I am very glad; Mr Giovanelli hasn't been near us since she was taken ill. I thought he was so much of a gentleman; but I don't call that very polite! A lady told me that he was afraid I was angry with him for taking Daisy round at night. Well, so I am; but I suppose he knows I'm a lady. I would scorn to scold him. Anyway, she says she's not engaged. I don't know why she wanted you to know; but she said to me three times – "Mind you tell Mr Winterbourne." And then she told me to ask if you remembered the time you went to that castle, in Switzerland. But I said I wouldn't give any such messages as that. Only, if she is not engaged, I'm sure I'm glad to know it.'

But, as Winterbourne had said, it mattered very little. A week after this the poor girl died; it had been a terrible case of the fever. Daisy's grave was in the little Protestant cemetery, in an angle of the wall of imperial Rome, beneath the cypresses[83] and the thick spring flowers. Winterbourne stood there beside it, with a number of other mourners; a number larger than the scandal excited by the young lady's career would have led you to expect.[84] Near him stood Giovanelli, who came nearer still before Winterbourne turned away. Giovanelli was very pale; on this occasion he had no flower in his button-hole;[85] he seemed to wish to say something. At last he said, 'She was the most beautiful young lady I ever saw, and the most amiable.' And then he added in a moment, 'And she was the most innocent.'

Winterbourne looked at him, and presently repeated his words, 'And the most innocent?'

'The most innocent!'

Winterbourne felt sore and angry. 'Why the devil,' he asked, 'did you take her to that fatal place?'

Mr Giovanelli's urbanity was apparently imperturbable. He looked on the ground a moment, and then he said, 'For myself, I had no fear; and she wanted to go.'

'That was no reason!' Winterbourne declared.

The subtle Roman again dropped his eyes. 'If she had lived I should have got nothing. She would never have married me, I am sure.'

'She would never have married you?'

'For a moment I hoped so. But no, I am sure.'

Winterbourne listened to him; he stood staring at the raw protuberance among the April daisies. When he turned away again Mr Giovanelli, with his light slow step, had retired.

Winterbourne almost immediately left Rome; but the following summer he again met his aunt, Mrs Costello, at Vevey. Mrs Costello was fond of Vevey. In the interval Winterbourne had often thought of Daisy Miller and her mystifying manners. One day he spoke of her to his aunt – said it was on his conscience that he had done her injustice.

'I am sure I don't know,' said Mrs Costello. 'How did your injustice affect her?'

'She sent me a message before her death which I didn't understand at the time. But I have understood it since. She would have appreciated one's esteem.'

'Is that a modest way,' asked Mrs Costello, 'of saying that she would have reciprocated one's affection?'

Winterbourne offered no answer to this question; but he presently said, 'You were right in that remark that you made last summer. I was booked to make a mistake. I have lived too long in foreign parts.'

Nevertheless, he went back to live at Geneva, whence there continue to come the most contradictory accounts of his motives of sojourn: a report that he is 'studying' hard – an intimation that he is much interested in a very clever foreign lady.

NOTES

In compiling these notes, I have tried to put the modern reader in the same position as the well-informed reader of the 1870s. James's allusions are seldom idle: for example, his reference to Cherbuliez's *Paule Méré* (p.79) is, I am sure, intended as a hint to the reader that Daisy is innocent.

I have offered translations of the foreign words and phrases: if good linguists find these superfluous they need not, of course, refer to them.

PATRICIA CRICK

NOTES

1. (p. 41) *bantling*: a small child.
2. (p. 41) *Leslie Stephen*: critic and literary historian (1832–1904), father of Virginia Woolf, and son-in-law (by his first marriage) of Thackeray. He was editor of *The Cornhill Magazine* from 1871 to 1882.
3. (p. 47) *Vevey*: a popular holiday and health resort of the period. Murray's *Handbook for Travellers in Switzerland* (1846) says of it: 'It is principally distinguished for the exceeding beauty of its situation, on the margin of the Lake Leman [i.e. Lake Geneva], at a point where the scenery of its banks is perhaps most beautiful.' The area provided the setting for Rousseau's *Julie, ou la nouvelle Héloïse*, and it may be that James deliberately introduces his heroine in this same setting because he wishes to remind us of Rousseau's belief that the innocence and contentment of 'natural' man have been destroyed by the conventions of 'civilized' society.
4. (p. 47) *pension*: boarding house.
5. (p. 47) *Newport*: the fashionable resort in Rhode Island, where Henry James spent part of his boyhood.
6. (p. 47) *Saratoga*: Saratoga Springs, in New York State, which Baedeker's guide (1893) describes as 'the most noted inland watering-place in the United States'.
7. (p. 47) *Trois Couronnes*: 'Three Crowns'. Murray's *Knapsack Guide for Travellers in Switzerland* (1864) describes it as 'close to the lake: first-class inn... charges not out of proportion with the comfort, but the traveller will frequently find it full, and the other inns are far inferior.' The hotel is still in existence, and still considered by many the best in Vevey.
8. (p. 47) *Ocean House*: a hotel in Newport, situated on Bellevue Avenue, which Baedeker's guide describes as 'one of the

best in Newport'. The original hotel building was burned
down in 1898.

9. (p. 47) *Congress Hall*: a hotel situated on Broadway, Saratoga
Springs. Having 1000 beds, it was considered very large at
this period.

10. (p. 48) *Dent du Midi*: a famous peak (10,778 ft) commanding
the Val d'Illiez.

11. (p. 48) *Castle of Chillon*: a picturesque edifice (built in 1238),
situated on an isolated rock in the lake and surrounded by
deep water, though connected to the shore by a wooden
bridge. It was used as a state prison, and many of the early
Protestant religious reformers were shut up there.

12. (p. 48) *Geneva*: situated at the south-western tip of Lake
Geneva, this city was the focal point of the Protestant Refor-
mation in the sixteenth century.

13. (p. 48) *camphor*: a strong-smelling substance, distilled from
plants, which was very popular for medicinal purposes
until well into the present century. It still constitutes one
of the main ingredients of inhalants for nasal congestion.

14. (p. 48) *the little metropolis of Calvinism*: John Calvin (1509–
64), the Protestant reformer, lived in Geneva during the
latter part of his life. His rather austere doctrines (such as
that of predestination) had a deep and lasting effect on the
life of that city. His influence on the Puritans, including
those who settled in New England, was also considerable.

15. (p. 49) *attaché*: a minor official attached to a foreign
embassy.

16. (p. 49) *spindleshanks*: long, thin legs.

17. (p. 49) *alpenstock*: a stick with a pointed iron tip used in
mountaineering.

18. (p. 52) *the Simplon*: one of the main mountain passes
between Switzerland and Italy. The first Simplon railway
tunnel wasn't opened until 1906; before then, travellers had
to go by *diligence* (stage coach). 'To those who have not
become hardened by use it is rather a nervous thing to see
the heavy *diligence* turn round the corners of the zigzags in
the face of precipices, with the reins of the five horses flying
loose, and the horses apparently under no control. The

horses, however, know the road, and, except in snow, an accident is seldom heard of.' (Murray's *Knapsack Guide*)

19. (p. 53) *a coquette*: a woman who constantly tries to attract men.

20. (p. 54) *Daisy Miller*: names are often significant in James. The daisy is a very common flower; it can also be seen as simple and unpretentious. The fact that it opens up in the presence of the sun suggests life-loving qualities. The surname Miller reminds us that Daisy's father has made his fortune by trade, which would make him socially unacceptable to some people. Then again, the miller's trade is not only an ancient one, but essential to the survival of society.

21. (p. 55) *cars*: railway carriages.

22. (p. 56) *ever so many:* The expression 'ever so', which Daisy uses three times in as many lines, was considered to be the hallmark of an uncultivated person.

23. (p. 57) *inconduite*: impropriety.

24. (p. 57) *flirt*: one who plays at courtship without serious intentions. Traditionally, this was an activity which was frowned upon, but at this period flirting was becoming fashionable in American society. As Daisy says on p. 99: 'I'm a fearful, frightful flirt! Did you ever hear of a nice girl that was not?'

25. (p. 58) *courier*: a servant engaged by travellers abroad – particularly by unaccompanied ladies – to act as guide and interpreter, and to make all the necessary travel and accommodation arrangements.

26. (p. 61) *furbelows*: frills. Dresses of the period often trailed along the ground.

27. (p. 61) *tournure*: bearing.

28. (p. 61) *rouleaux*: ringlets.

29. (p. 63) *Tout bonnement!* Simply!

30. (p. 66) *comme il faut*: correct.

31. (p. 66) *table d'hôte*: nowadays this simply means a set menu, but originally the expression referred to the common table at a hotel or inn, and to meals at set times. *Table d'hôte* meals at the Trois Couronnes in the 1870s were served at 1 p.m., 5 p.m., and 7.30 p.m. The alternative, having meals served in one's rooms, was naturally more expensive.

32. (p. 71) *the dark old city at the other end of the lake*: although we never actually visit Geneva, its presence – here seen as rather brooding and ominous – is constantly being evoked.
33. (p. 72) *chaffing*: teasing.
34. (p. 75) *what metaphysicians term the objective cast*: an example of James's circumlocutory style at its most irritating. In the New York edition we find: 'Her discourse was for the most part of what immediately and superficially surrounded them.'
35. (p. 75) *You look as if you were taking me to a funeral*: a forewarning of the final outcome of their relationship.
36. (p. 76) *flirted*: darted (another meaning of the word).
37. (p. 76) *oubliettes*: dungeons into which prisoners were thrown and, as the name implies, forgotten. The *oubliette* at Chillon (there is apparently only one) has a single entrance: a trap-door in the floor above. The unlucky prisoner would begin to descend what looked like a spiral staircase; however, after a few steps the staircase stopped, so that he would fall, in the darkness, to the dungeon eighty feet below.
38. (p. 76) *Bonnivard*: 1496–1571? supported Geneva's claim to be a republic, and was imprisoned in Chillon for six years by the Duke of Savoy. Byron's *Prisoner of Chillon* was popularly assumed to be telling the story of Bonnivard, but in fact Byron was unacquainted with his history at the time of writing this poem. *His* prisoner is an anonymous captive who has been immured for his religious beliefs. However in his later 'Sonnet on Chillon', Byron wrote:

> Chillon! thy prison is a holy place,
> And thy sad floor an altar – for 'twas trod,
> Until his very steps have left a trace
> Worn, as if thy cold pavement were a sod,
> By Bonnivard!

39. (p. 78) *persiflage*: mockery.
40. (p. 78) *invidious*: showing unjust discrimination. It isn't clear, however, whether this is the author's or Winterbourne's own judgement on his aunt's attitude to Daisy.
41. (p. 79) *intime*: 'intimate'.

42. (p. 79) *that pretty novel of Cherbuliez's: Paule Méré*. This novel, first published in book form in 1865 (is James trying to tell us that Mrs Costello is rather out-of-date?), has striking parallels with the present story. The heroine, who is essentially innocent but rather unconventional, has her reputation blackened by the malicious gossip of Genevan society. The hero, who loves her, tries to ignore the gossip; nevertheless, it ultimately destroys their relationship. As one of the characters remarks at the end of the novel, 'What is this weakness which makes us listen to a society which we despise?' Mrs Costello seems totally unaware of the relevance of *Paule Méré* to the present situation – but James surely meant his readers to be aware of it.

43. (p. 82) *the dyspepsia*: Murray's *Handbook of Rome* (1867) states: 'Rome is very injurious in what is generally known by the designation of *weak stomachs*: and it is particularly prejudicial in cases of *atonic dyspepsia* and hypochondriacal affections' (i.e. affections of the liver, gall-bladder, and spleen).

44. (p. 82) *the infant Hannibal*: Hannibal (247–182 B C), the Carthaginian general, was an implacable enemy of Rome.

45. (p. 83) *Zürich*: this town is indeed remarkable for its scenic situation; it may also have appealed to Mrs Miller as the most important Swiss manufacturing town.

46. (p. 83) *had stopped neither at Bologna nor at Florence*: for a cultured traveller like Winterbourne to sacrifice a visit to these centres of learning and culture does indeed show his impatience. However, as on other occasions, he does not express these thoughts to Daisy – if he did, the outcome might be very different.

47. (p. 84) *quaint*: Daisy obviously finds his choice of words old-fashioned and over-formal.

48. (p. 84) *raise something*: Cain, perhaps, or hell. Even Randolph is aware that there are some expressions one doesn't use in polite society.

49. (p. 84) *Giovanelli*: the name means 'young man'. Are we meant to see him as a type?

50. (p. 85) *You'll get the fever*: 'Roman fever' (malaria) was endemic until the draining of the Pontine marshes was completed in the 1930s. The nature of the disease, which is

carried by mosquitoes, was imperfectly understood until the 1890s. It was thought to be caused, as the name 'malaria' implies, by 'bad air', or 'miasmas'. 'Chills in damp places' (among many other, less relevant warnings) are cited by Murray's *Handbook of Rome* as a predisposing cause. The same source tells us that 'the couriers who carried the mails at all seasons between Rome and Naples made it a rule not to sleep whilst crossing the Pontine marshes, and generally *smoked* [my italics] as an additional security'. It sounds as though the couriers had very nearly stumbled on the truth!

51. (p. 85) *Your friend won't keep you from getting the fever*: another premonition of the final tragedy.

52. (p. 88) *a glass in one eye*: i.e. a monocle.

53. (p. 88) *a nosegay in his button-hole*: in James's novels, an over-exuberant button-hole is the sign of someone who is not quite a gentleman.

54. (p. 89) *a penny-a-liner*: a freelance journalist or author paid by the line, i.e. not one of any great importance.

55. (p. 90) *a presumably low-lived foreigner*: James probably means 'low-living'. Note the prejudice against foreigners, typical of even educated Anglo-Saxons of this period.

56. (p. 90) *amoroso*: sweetheart.

57. (p. 90) *the revolving train*: the carriages driving round the Pincio. It was the custom in society to take a drive in the late afternoon.

58. (p. 92) *victoria*: a four-wheeled carriage with a folding hood.

59. (p. 97) *Elle s'affiche*: She's making a spectacle of herself.

60. (p. 99) *It seems to me much more proper in young unmarried women than in old married ones*: the twentieth-century reader will probably agree with Daisy.

61. (p. 103) *Miss Baker's, Miss Chandler's*: Mrs Costello probably remembers Daisy's surname perfectly well; she is deliberately sneering at her social origins.

62. (p. 103) *intrigue*: secret love affair.

63. (p. 103) *barber's block*: a stand on which wigs are made and displayed. The implication is that Giovanelli is just a handsome face.

64. (p. 103) *as they did in the Golden Age*: in Greek and Roman myth, the Golden Age was the first age of the world, in

which everyone was happy and innocent. We are reminded of Rousseau again.

65. (p. 103) *cavaliere avvocato*: lawyer.

66. (p. 104) *marchese*: marquis.

67. (p. 104) *qui se passe ses fantaisies*: who does what she likes.

68. (p. 104) *vesper-service*: evening service.

69. (p. 105) *Innocent X by Velazquez*: the name of this pope is perhaps a reminder of Daisy's own innocence.

70. (p. 105) *du meilleur monde*: of the best society.

71. (p. 109) *cicerone*: guide.

72. (p. 110) *the Colosseum*: the great amphitheatre, constructed in the first century A D, in which gladiatorial combats were held and (according to tradition) many early Christians were thrown to wild beasts. It isn't unusual in James for significant episodes to take place in the Colosseum (see, for example, *Roderick Hudson* or *Portrait of a Lady*).

73. (p. 110) *Byron's famous lines*: in Byron's play *Manfred* there is a long opening passage to Act 3 scene 4 in which Manfred describes the Colosseum by moonlight. The passage ends:

> And thou didst shine, thou rolling moon, upon
> All this, and cast a wide and tender light,
> Which softened down the hoar austerity
> Of rugged desolation, and fill'd up
> As 'twere anew, the gaps of centuries;
> Leaving that beautiful which still was so,
> And making that which was not, till the place
> Became religion, and the heart ran o'er
> With silent worship of the great of old:-
> The dead but scepter'd sovereigns, who still rule
> Our spirits from their urns.

74. (p. 110) *deprecated by the doctors*: because it was realized that visiting deserted places at night was likely to lead to malaria.

75. (p. 110) *the great cross in the centre*: erected in memory of the Christian martyrs.

76. (p. 111) *he cuts me*: for a gentleman to 'cut' (decline to acknowledge) a lady would be deeply insulting. Winterbourne, of course, didn't intend to do this: he doesn't realize that Daisy has recognized him.

77. (p. 111) *perniciosa*: another name for malaria.
78. (p. 112) *He has got some splendid pills*: probably quinine, which was used in the treatment of malaria.
79. (p. 112) *That's one good thing*: Daisy implies that she has otherwise been disappointed in her visit to Rome.
80. (p. 113) *If we get in by midnight we are quite safe*: this indicates the kind of folklore, part superstition, part based on observation, which surrounded Roman fever.
81. (p. 113) *I don't care . . . whether I have Roman fever or not*: arguably, it is as much Winterbourne's attitude to her, as Daisy's own folly, which kills her. Note that this remark echoes his last one to her.
82. (p. 113) *desultory*: i.e. incomplete.
83. (p. 115) *the cypresses*: Italian cemeteries are traditionally planted with these trees.
84. (p. 115) *a number larger than the scandal excited by the young lady's career would have led you to expect*: perhaps because in fact people had not been as scandalized as they made out.
85. (p. 115) *on this occasion he had no flower in his button-hole*: because he is in mourning for Daisy.

PENGUIN BOOKS — GREAT IDEAS

The First Ten Books

Confucius

551–479 BC

Confucius

The First Ten Books

TRANSLATED BY
D. C. LAU

PENGUIN BOOKS — GREAT IDEAS

PENGUIN BOOKS

Published by the Penguin Group
Penguin Books Ltd, 80 Strand, London WC2R ORL, England
Penguin Group (USA) Inc., 375 Hudson Street, New York, New York 10014, USA
Penguin Group (Canada), 10 Alcorn Avenue, Toronto, Ontario, Canada M4V 3B2
(a division of Pearson Penguin Canada Inc.)
Penguin Ireland, 25 St Stephen's Green, Dublin 2, Ireland
(a division of Penguin Books Ltd)
Penguin Group (Australia), 250 Camberwell Road,
Camberwell, Victoria 3124, Australia (a division of Pearson Australia Group Pty Ltd)
Penguin Books India Pvt Ltd, 11 Community Centre,
Panchsheel Park, New Delhi – 110 017, India
Penguin Group (NZ), cnr Airborne and Rosedale Roads, Albany,
Auckland 1310, New Zealand (a division of Pearson New Zealand Ltd)
Penguin Books (South Africa) (Pty) Ltd, 24 Sturdee Avenue,
Rosebank 2196, South Africa

Penguin Books Ltd, Registered Offices: 80 Strand, London WC2R ORL, England

www.penguin.com

The Analects first published in Penguin Classics 1979
This extract published in Penguin Books 2005

8

Translation copyright © D. C. Lau, 1979

Taken from the Penguin Classics edition of *The Analects*,
translated and introduced by D. C. Lau

Set by Rowland Phototypesetting Ltd, Bury St Edmunds, Suffolk
Printed in England by Clays Ltd, St Ives plc

ISBN-13: 978-0-14-102380-9

www.greenpenguin.co.uk

Penguin Books is committed to a sustainable future
for our business, our readers and our planet.
The book in your hands is made from paper
certified by the Forest Stewardship Council.

Contents

Book I

1. The Master said, 'Is it not a pleasure, having learned something, to try it out at due intervals? Is it not a joy to have friends come from afar? Is it not gentlemanly not to take offence when others fail to appreciate your abilities?'

2. Yu Tzu said, 'It is rare for a man whose character is such that he is good as a son and obedient as a young man to have the inclination to transgress against his superiors; it is unheard of for one who has no such inclination to be inclined to start a rebellion. The gentleman devotes his efforts to the roots, for once the roots are established, the Way will grow therefrom. Being good as a son and obedient as a young man is, perhaps, the root of a man's character.'

3. The Master said, 'It is rare, indeed, for a man with cunning words and an ingratiating face to be benevolent.'

4. Tseng Tzu said, 'Every day I examine myself on three counts. In what I have undertaken on another's behalf, have I failed to do my best? In my dealings with my friends have I failed to be trustworthy in what I say? Have I passed on to others anything that I have not tried out myself?'

5. The Master said, 'In guiding a state of a thousand chariots, approach your duties with reverence and be

trustworthy in what you say; avoid excesses in expenditure and love your fellow men; employ the labour of the common people only in the right seasons.'

6. The Master said, 'A young man should be a good son at home and an obedient young man abroad, sparing of speech but trustworthy in what he says, and should love the multitude at large but cultivate the friendship of his fellow men. If he has any energy to spare from such action, let him devote it to making himself cultivated.'

7. Tzu-hsia said, 'I would grant that a man has received instruction who appreciates men of excellence where other men appreciate beautiful women, who exerts himself to the utmost in the service of his parents and offers his person to the service of his lord, and who, in his dealings with his friends, is trustworthy in what he says, even though he may say that he has never been taught.'

8. The Master said, 'A gentleman who lacks gravity does not inspire awe. A gentleman who studies is unlikely to be inflexible.

'Make* it your guiding principle to do your best for others and to be trustworthy in what you say. Do not accept as friend anyone who is not as good as you.

'When you make a mistake, do not be afraid of mending your ways.'

9. Tseng Tzu said, 'Conduct the funeral of your parents with meticulous care and let not sacrifices to your remote

---

* The whole of what follows is found also in IX.25.

ancestors be forgotten, and the virtue of the common people will incline towards fullness.'

10. Tzu-ch'in asked Tzu-kung, 'When the Master arrives in a state, he invariably gets to know about its government. Does he seek this information? or is it given him?'

Tzu-kung said, 'The Master gets it through being cordial, good, respectful, frugal and deferential. The way the Master seeks it is, perhaps, different from the way other men seek it.'

11. The Master said, 'Observe what a man has in mind to do when his father is living, and then observe what he does when his father is dead. If, for three years, he makes no changes to his father's ways, he can be said to be a good son.'*

12. Yu Tzu said, 'Of the things brought about by the rites, harmony is the most valuable. Of the ways of the Former Kings, this is the most beautiful, and is followed alike in matters great and small, yet this will not always work: to aim always at harmony without regulating it by the rites simply because one knows only about harmony will not, in fact, work.'

13. Yu Tzu said, 'To be trustworthy in word is close to being moral in that it enables one's words to be repeated. To be respectful is close to being observant of the rites in that it enables one to stay clear of disgrace and insult. If, in promoting good relationship with relatives by marriage, a man manages not to lose the good will of

* This sentence is found again in IV.20.

his own kinsmen, he is worthy of being looked up to as the head of the clan.'

14. The Master said, 'The gentleman seeks neither a full belly nor a comfortable home. He is quick in action but cautious in speech. He goes to men possessed of the Way to be put right. Such a man can be described as eager to learn.'

15. Tzu-kung said, ' "Poor without being obsequious, wealthy without being arrogant." What do you think of this saying?'

The Master said, 'That will do, but better still "Poor yet delighting in the Way, wealthy yet observant of the rites." '

Tzu-kung said, 'The *Odes* say,

> Like bone cut, like horn polished,
> Like jade carved, like stone ground.

Is not what you have said a case in point?'

16. The Master said, 'Ssu, only with a man like you can one discuss the *Odes*. Tell such a man something and he can see its relevance to what he has not been told.'

The Master said, 'It is not the failure of others to appreciate your abilities that should trouble you, but rather your failure to appreciate theirs.'

Book II

1. The Master said, 'The rule of virtue can be compared to the Pole Star which commands the homage of the multitude of stars without leaving its place.'

2. The Master said, 'The *Odes* are three hundred in number. They can be summed up in one phrase,

> Swerving not from the right path.'*

3. The Master said, 'Guide them by edicts, keep them in line with punishments, and the common people will stay out of trouble but will have no sense of shame. Guide them by virtue, keep them in line with the rites, and they will, besides having a sense of shame, reform themselves.'

4. The Master said, 'At fifteen I set my heart on learning; at thirty I took my stand; at forty I came to be free from doubts; at fifty I understood the Decree of Heaven; at sixty my ear was atuned;† at seventy I followed my heart's desire without overstepping the line.'

---

* This line is from Ode 297 where it describes a team of horses going straight ahead without swerving to left or right.
† The expression *erh shun* is very obscure and the translation is tentative.

5. Meng Yi Tzu asked about being filial. The Master answered, 'Never fail to comply.'

Fan Ch'ih was driving. The Master told him about the interview, saying, 'Meng-sun asked me about being filial. I answered, "Never fail to comply."'

Fan Ch'ih asked, 'What does that mean?'

The Master said, 'When your parents are alive, comply with the rites in serving them; when they die, comply with the rites in burying them; comply with the rites in sacrificing to them.'

6. Meng Wu Po asked about being filial. The Master said, 'Give your father and mother no other cause for anxiety than illness.'

7. Tzu-yu asked about being filial. The Master said, 'Nowadays for a man to be filial means no more than that he is able to provide his parents with food. Even hounds and horses are, in some way, provided with food. If a man shows no reverence, where is the difference?'

8. Tzu-hsia asked about being filial. The Master said, 'What is difficult to manage is the expression on one's face. As for the young taking on the burden when there is work to be done or letting the old enjoy the wine and the food when these are available, that hardly deserves to be called filial.'

9. The Master said, 'I can speak to Hui all day without his disagreeing with me in any way. Thus he would seem to be stupid. However, when I take a closer look at what he does in private after he has withdrawn from my

presence, I discover that it does, in fact, throw light on what I said. Hui is not stupid after all.'

10. The Master said, 'Look at the means a man employs, observe the path he takes and examine where he feels at home. In what way is a man's true character hidden from view? In what way is a man's true character hidden from view?'

11. The Master said, 'A man is worthy of being a teacher who gets to know what is new by keeping fresh in his mind what he is already familiar with.'

12. The Master said, 'The gentleman is no vessel.'*

13. Tzu-kung asked about the gentleman. The Master said, 'He puts his words into action before allowing his words to follow his action.'

14. The Master said, 'The gentleman enters into associations but not cliques; the small man enters into cliques but not associations.'

15. The Master said, 'If one learns from others but does not think, one will be bewildered. If, on the other hand, one thinks but does not learn from others, one will be in peril.'

16. The Master said, 'To attack a task from the wrong end can do nothing but harm.'

17. The Master said, 'Yu, shall I tell you what it is to

---

*i.e., he is no specialist, as every vessel is designed for a specific purpose only.

know. To say you know when you know, and to say you do not when you do not, that is knowledge.'

18. Tzu-chang was studying with an eye to an official career. The Master said, 'Use your ears widely but leave out what is doubtful; repeat the rest with caution and you will make few mistakes. Use your eyes widely and leave out what is hazardous; put the rest into practice with caution and you will have few regrets. When in your speech you make few mistakes and in your action you have few regrets, an official career will follow as a matter of course.'

19. Duke Ai asked, 'What must I do before the common people will look up to me?'

Confucius answered, 'Raise the straight and set them over the crooked and the common people will look up to you. Raise the crooked and set them over the straight and the common people will not look up to you.'

20. Chi K'ang Tzu asked, 'How can one inculcate in the common people the virtue of reverence, of doing their best and of enthusiasm?'

The Master said, 'Rule over them with dignity and they will be reverent; treat them with kindness and they will do their best; raise the good and instruct those who are backward and they will be imbued with enthusiasm.'

21. Someone said to Confucius, 'Why do you not take part in government?'

The Master said, 'The *Book of History* says, "Oh! Simply by being a good son and friendly to his brothers a man can exert an influence upon government." In so doing a man is, in fact, taking part in government. How can there be any question of his having actively to "take part in government"?'

22. The Master said, 'I do not see how a man can be acceptable who is untrustworthy in word. When a pin is missing in the yoke-bar of a large cart or in the collar-bar of a small cart, how can the cart be expected to go?'

23. Tzu-chang asked, 'Can ten generations hence be known?'

The Master said, 'The Yin built on the rites of the Hsia. What was added and what was omitted can be known. The Chou built on the rites of the Yin. What was added and what was omitted can be known. Should there be a successor to the Chou, even a hundred generations hence can be known.'

24. The Master said, 'To offer sacrifice to the spirit of an ancestor not one's own is obsequious.

'Faced with what is right, to leave it undone shows a lack of courage.'

Book III

1. Confucius said of the Chi Family, 'They use eight rows of eight dancers each* to perform in their courtyard. If this can be tolerated, what cannot be tolerated?'

2. The Three Families† performed the *yung*‡ when the sacrificial offerings were being cleared away. The Master said,

> 'In attendance were the great lords,
> In solemn dignity was the Emperor.

What application has this to the halls of the Three Families?'

3. The Master said, 'What can a man do with the rites who is not benevolent? What can a man do with music who is not benevolent?'

4. Lin Fang asked about the basis of the rites. The Master said, 'A noble question indeed! With the rites, it is better to err on the side of frugality than on the side of extrava-

---

* A prerogative of the Emperor.
† The three noble families of the state of Lu: Meng-sun, Shu-sun and Chi-sun.
‡ Ode 282, from which the couplet quoted comes.

gance; in mourning, it is better to err on the side of grief than on the side of formality.'

5. The Master said, 'Barbarian tribes with their rulers are inferior to Chinese states without them.'

6. The Chi Family were going to perform the sacrifice to Mount T'ai.* The Master said to Jan Ch'iu,† 'Can you not save the situation?'

'No. I cannot.'

The Master said, 'Alas! Who would have thought that Mount T'ai would suffer in comparison with Lin Fang?'‡

7. The Master said, 'There is no contention between gentlemen. The nearest to it is, perhaps, archery. In archery they bow and make way for one another as they go up and on coming down they drink together. Even the way they contend is gentlemanly.'

8. Tzu-hsia asked,

> 'Her entrancing smile dimpling,
> Her beautiful eyes glancing,
> Patterns of colour upon plain silk.

What is the meaning of these lines?'

---

* Not being the lord of the state of Lu, the head of the Chi Family was not entitled to perform the sacrifice to Mount T'ai and it would be a violation of the rites for Mount T'ai to accept the sacrifice.
† Who was in the service of the Chi Family.
‡ See III.4 above where Lin Fang showed a concern for the basis of the rites.

The Master said, 'The colours are put in after the white.'

'Does the practice of the rites likewise come afterwards?'

The Master said, 'It is you, Shang, who have thrown light on the text for me. Only with a man like you can one discuss the *Odes*.'

9. The Master said, 'I am able to discourse on the rites of the Hsia, but the state of Ch'i does not furnish sufficient supporting evidence; I am able to discourse on the rites of the Yin, but the state of Sung does not furnish sufficient supporting evidence. This is because there are not enough records and men of erudition. Otherwise I would be able to support what I say with evidence.'

10. The Master said, 'I do not wish to witness that part of the *ti* sacrifice* which follows the opening libation to the impersonator.'†

11. Someone asked about the theory of the *ti* sacrifice. The Master said, 'It is not something I understand, for whoever understands it will be able to manage the Empire as easily as if he had it here,' pointing to his palm.

12. 'Sacrifice as if present' is taken to mean 'sacrifice to the gods as if the gods were present.'

---

* An important sacrifice performed by the Emperor, but the privilege of performing it was granted to the Duke of Chou, the founder of the state of Lu.

† The young boy or girl who impersonates the dead ancestor to whom the offerings are made.

The Master, however, said, 'Unless I take part in a sacrifice, it is as if I did not sacrifice.'

13. Wang-sun Chia said,

> 'Better to be obsequious to the kitchen stove
> Than to the south-west corner of the house.*

What does that mean?'

The Master said, 'The saying has got it wrong. When you have offended against Heaven, there is nowhere you can turn to in your prayers.'

14. The Master said, 'The Chou is resplendent in culture, having before it the example of the two previous dynasties.† I am for the Chou.'

15. When the Master went inside the Grand Temple,‡ he asked questions about everything. Someone remarked, 'Who said that the son of the man from Tsou§ understood the rites? When he went inside the Grand Temple, he asked questions about everything.'

The Master, on hearing of this, said, 'The asking of questions is in itself the correct rite.'

16. The Master said,

---

* By 'the south-west corner of the house', which is the place of honour, Wang-sun Chia, being a minister of Wei, presumably meant to refer to the lord of Wei and by 'the kitchen stove' to himself.
† The Hsia and the Yin.
‡ The temple of the Duke of Chou, the founder of the state of Lu.
§ The man from Tsou refers to Confucius' father.

'In archery the point lies not in piercing the hide,*
For the reason that strength varies from man to man.

This was the way of antiquity.'

17. Tzu-kung wanted to do away with the sacrificial sheep at the announcement of the new moon. The Master said, 'Ssu, you are loath to part with the price of the sheep, but I am loath to see the disappearance of the rite.'

18. The Master said, 'You will be looked upon as obsequious by others if you observe every detail of the rites in serving your lord.'

19. Duke Ting asked, 'What is the way the ruler should employ the services of his subjects? What is the way a subject should serve his ruler?'

Confucius answered, 'The ruler should employ the services of his subjects in accordance with the rites. A subject should serve his ruler by doing his best.'

20. The Master said, 'In the *kuan chü*† there is joy without wantonness, and sorrow without self-injury.'

21. Duke Ai asked Tsai Wo about the altar to the god of earth. Tsai Wo replied, 'The Hsia used the pine, the Yin used the cedar, and the men of Chou used the chestnut (*li*), saying that it made the common people tremble (*li*).'

The Master, on hearing of this reply, commented, 'One does not explain away what is already done, one

---

* i.e., the bull's eye fixed in the centre of a cloth target.
† The first ode in the *Odes*.

does not argue against what is already accomplished, and one does not condemn what has already gone by.'

22. The Master said, 'Kuan Chung was, indeed, a vessel of small capacity.'

Someone remarked, 'Was Kuan Chung frugal, then?'

'Kuan Chung kept three separate establishments, each complete with its own staff. How can he be called frugal?'

'In that case, did Kuan Chung understand the rites?'

'Rulers of states erect gate-screens; Kuan Chung erected such a screen as well. The ruler of a state, when entertaining the ruler of another state, has a stand for inverted cups; Kuan Chung had such a stand as well. If even Kuan Chung understood the rites, who does not understand them?'

23. The Master talked of music to the Grand Musician of Lu, saying, 'This much can be known about music. It begins with playing in unison. When it gets into full swing, it is harmonious, clear and unbroken. In this way it reaches the conclusion.'

24. The border official of Yi requested an audience, saying, 'I have never been denied an audience by any gentleman who has come to this place.' The followers presented him. When he came out, he said, 'What worry have you, gentlemen, about the loss of office? The Empire has long been without the Way. Heaven is about to use your Master as the wooden tongue for a bell.'*

---

* To rouse the Empire.

25. The Master said of the *shao** that it was both perfectly beautiful and perfectly good, and of the *wu*† that it was perfectly beautiful but not perfectly good.

26. The Master said, 'What can I find worthy of note in a man who is lacking in tolerance when in high position, in reverence when performing the rites and in sorrow when in mourning?'

---

* The music of Shun who came to the throne through the abdication of Yao.
† The music of King Wu who came to the throne through overthrowing the Yin by military force.

Book IV

1. The Master said, 'Of neighbourhoods benevolence is the most beautiful. How can the man be considered wise who, when he has the choice, does not settle in benevolence?'

2. The Master said, 'One who is not benevolent cannot remain long in straitened circumstances, nor can he remain long in easy circumstances.

'The benevolent man is attracted to benevolence because he feels at home in it. The wise man is attracted to benevolence because he finds it to his advantage.'

3. The Master said, 'It is only the benevolent man who is capable of liking or disliking other men.'

4. The Master said, 'If a man sets his heart on benevolence, he will be free from evil.'

5. The Master said, 'Wealth and high station are what men desire but unless I got them in the right way I would not remain in them. Poverty and low station are what men dislike, but even if I did not get them in the right way I would not try to escape from them.*

* This sentence is most likely to be corrupt. The negative is probably an interpolation and the sentence should read: 'Poverty and low station are what men dislike, but if I got them in the right way I would not try to escape from them.'

'If the gentleman forsakes benevolence, in what way can he make a name for himself? The gentleman never deserts benevolence, not even for as long as it takes to eat a meal. If he hurries and stumbles one may be sure that it is in benevolence that he does so.'

6. The Master said, 'I have never met a man who finds benevolence attractive or a man who finds unbenevolence* repulsive. A man who finds benevolence attractive cannot be surpassed. A man who finds unbenevolence repulsive can, perhaps, be counted as benevolent, for he would not allow what is not benevolent to contaminate his person.

'Is there a man who, for the space of a single day, is able to devote all his strength to benevolence? I have not come across such a man whose strength proves insufficient for the task. There must be such cases of insufficient strength, only I have not come across them.'

7. The Master said, 'In his errors a man is true to type. Observe the errors and you will know the man.'

8. The Master said, 'He has not lived in vain who dies the day he is told about the Way.'

9. The Master said, 'There is no point in seeking the views of a Gentleman who, though he sets his heart on the Way, is ashamed of poor food and poor clothes.'

10. The Master said, 'In his dealings with the world the

---

* The word 'unbenevolence' has been coined because the original word has a positive meaning lacking in 'non-benevolence'.

gentleman is not invariably for or against anything. He is on the side of what is moral.'

11. The Master said, 'While the gentleman cherishes benign rule, the small man cherishes his native land. While the gentleman cherishes a respect for the law, the small man cherishes generous treatment.'*

12. The Master said, 'If one is guided by profit in one's actions, one will incur much ill will.'

13. The Master said, 'If a man is able to govern a state by observing the rites and showing deference, what difficulties will he have in public life? If he is unable to govern a state by observing the rites and showing deference, what good are the rites to him?'

14. The Master said, 'Do not worry because you have no official position. Worry about your qualifications. Do not worry because no one appreciates your abilities. Seek to be worthy of appreciation.'

15. The Master said, 'Ts'an! There is one single thread binding my way together.'

Tseng Tzu assented.

After the Master had gone out, the disciples asked, 'What did he mean?'

Tseng Tzu said, 'The way of the Master consists in doing one's best and in using oneself as a measure to gauge others. That is all.'

* The distinction here between 'the gentleman' and 'the small man' is not, as is often the case, drawn between the ruler and the ruled but within the class of the ruled.

16. The Master said, 'The gentleman understands what is moral. The small man understands what is profitable.'

17. The Master said, 'When you meet someone better than yourself, turn your thoughts to becoming his equal. When you meet someone not as good as you are, look within and examine your own self.'

18. The Master said, 'In serving your father and mother you ought to dissuade them from doing wrong in the gentlest way. If you see your advice being ignored, you should not become disobedient but remain reverent. You should not complain even if in so doing you wear yourself out.'

19. The Master said, 'While your parents are alive, you should not go too far afield in your travels. If you do, your whereabouts should always be known.'

20. The Master said, 'If, for three years, a man makes no changes to his father's ways, he can be said to be a good son.'

21. The Master said, 'A man should not be ignorant of the age of his father and mother. It is a matter, on the one hand, for rejoicing and, on the other, for anxiety.'

22. The Master said, 'In antiquity men were loath to speak. This was because they counted it shameful if their person failed to keep up with their words.'

23. The Master said, 'It is rare for a man to miss the mark through holding on to essentials.'

24. The Master said, 'The gentleman desires to be halting in speech but quick in action.'

25. The Master said, 'Virtue never stands alone. It is bound to have neighbours.'

26. Tzu-yu said, 'To be importunate with one's lord will mean humiliation. To be importunate with one's friends will mean estrangement.'

Book V

1. The Master said of Kung-yeh Ch'ang that he was a suitable choice for a husband, for though he was in gaol it was not as though he had done anything wrong. He gave him his daughter in marriage.

2. The Master said of Nan-jung that when the Way prevailed in the state he was not cast aside and when the Way fell into disuse he stayed clear of the humiliation of punishment. He gave him his elder brother's daughter in marriage.

3. The Master's comment on Tzu-chien was 'What a gentleman this man is! If there were no gentlemen in Lu where could he have acquired his qualities?'

4. Tzu-kung asked, 'What do you think of me?'
   The Master said, 'You are a vessel.'
   'What kind of vessel?'
   'A sacrificial vessel.'*

5. Someone said, 'Yung is benevolent but does not have a facile tongue.'
   The Master said, 'What need is there for him to have a facile tongue? For a man quick with a retort there are frequent occasions on which he will incur the hatred of

* Made of jade.

22

others. I cannot say whether Yung is benevolent or not, but what need is there for him to have a facile tongue?'

6. The Master told Ch'i-tiao K'ai to take office. Ch'i-tiao K'ai said, 'I cannot trust myself to do so yet.' The Master was pleased.

7. The Master said, 'If the Way should fail to prevail and I were to put to sea on a raft, the one who would follow me would no doubt be Yu.' Tzu-lu, on hearing this, was overjoyed. The Master said, 'Yu has a greater love for courage than I, but is lacking in judgement.'

8. Meng Wu Po asked whether Tzu-lu was benevolent. The Master said, 'I cannot say.' Meng Wu Po repeated the question. The Master said, 'Yu can be given the responsibility of managing the military levies in a state of a thousand chariots, but whether he is benevolent or not I cannot say.'

'What about Ch'iu?'

The Master said, 'Ch'iu can be given the responsibility as a steward in a town with a thousand households or in a noble family with a hundred chariots, but whether he is benevolent or not I cannot say.'

'What about Ch'ih?'

The Master said, 'When Ch'ih, putting on his sash, takes his place at court, he can be given the responsibility of conversing with the guests, but whether he is benevolent or not I cannot say.'

9. The Master said to Tzu-kung, 'Who is the better man, you or Hui?'

'How dare I compare myself with Hui? When he is

told one thing he understands ten. When I am told one thing I understand only two.'

The Master said, 'You are not as good as he is. Neither of us is as good as he is.'

10. Tsai Yü was in bed in the daytime. The Master said, 'A piece of rotten wood cannot be carved, nor can a wall of dried dung be trowelled. As far as Yü is concerned what is the use of condemning him?' The Master added, 'I used to take on trust a man's deeds after having listened to his words. Now having listened to a man's words I go on to observe his deeds. It was on account of Yü that I have changed in this respect.'

11. The Master said, 'I have never met anyone who is truly unbending.'

Someone said, 'What about Shen Ch'eng?'

The Master said, 'Ch'eng is full of desires. How can he be unbending?'

12. Tzu-kung said, 'While I do not wish others to impose on me, I also wish not to impose on others.'

The Master said, 'Ssu, that is quite beyond you.'

13. Tzu-kung said, 'One can get to hear about the Master's accomplishments, but one cannot get to hear his views on human nature and the Way of Heaven.'

14. Before he could put into practice something he had heard, the only thing Tzu-lu feared was that he should be told something further.

15. Tzu-kung asked, 'Why was K'ung Wen Tzu called "wen"?'

The Master said, 'He was quick and eager to learn: he was not ashamed to seek the advice of those who were beneath him in station. That is why he was called "wen".'

16. The Master said of Tzu-ch'an that he had the way of the gentleman on four counts: he was respectful in the manner he conducted himself; he was reverent in the service of his lord; in caring for the common people, he was generous and, in employing their services, he was just.

17. The Master said, 'Yen P'ing-chung excelled in friendship: even after long acquaintance he treated his friends with reverence.'

18. The Master said, 'When housing his great tortoise, Tsang Wen-chung had the capitals of the pillars carved in the shape of hills and the rafterposts painted in a duck-weed design. What is one to think of his intelligence?'

19. Tzu-chang asked, 'Ling Yin* Tzu-wen gave no appearance of pleasure when he was made prime minister three times. Neither did he give any appearance of displeasure when he was removed from office three times. He always told his successor what he had done during his term of office. What do you think of this?'

The Master said, 'He can, indeed, be said to be a man who does his best.'

'Can he be said to be benevolent?'

'He cannot even be said to be wise. How can he be said to be benevolent?'

* This was the title in the state of Ch'u for the prime minister.

'When Ts'ui Tzu assassinated the Lord of Ch'i, Ch'en Wen Tzu who owned ten teams of four horses each abandoned them and left the state. On arriving in another state, he said, "The officials here are no better than our Counsellor Ts'ui Tzu." He left and went to yet another state. Once more, he said, "The officials here are no better than our Counsellor Ts'ui Tzu," and he again left. What do you think of this?'

The Master said, 'He can, indeed, be said to be pure.'

'Can he be said to be benevolent?'

'He cannot even be said to be wise. How can he be said to be benevolent?'

20. Chi Wen Tzu always thought three times before taking action. When the Master was told of this, he commented, 'Twice is quite enough.'

21. The Master said, 'Ning Wu Tzu was intelligent when the Way prevailed in the state, but stupid when it did not. Others may equal his intelligence but they cannot equal his stupidity.'

22. When he was in Ch'en, the Master said, 'Let us go home. Let us go home. Our young men at home are wildly ambitious, and have great accomplishments for all to see, but they do not know how to prune themselves.'

23. The Master said, 'Po Yi and Shu Ch'i never remembered old scores. For this reason they incurred little ill will.'

24. The Master said, 'Who said Wei-sheng Kao was straight? Once when someone begged him for vinegar,

he went and begged it off a neighbour to give it to him.'

25. The Master said, 'Cunning words, an ingratiating face and utter servility, these things Tso-ch'iu Ming found shameful. I, too, find them shameful. To be friendly towards someone while concealing one's hostility, this Tso-ch'iu Ming found shameful. I, too, find it shameful.'

26. Yen Yüan and Chi-lu were in attendance. The Master said, 'I suggest you each tell me what it is you have set your hearts on.'

Tzu-lu said, 'I should like to share my carriage and horses, clothes and furs with my friends, and to have no regrets even if they become worn.'

Yen Yüan said, 'I should like never to boast of my own goodness and never to impose onerous tasks upon others.'

Tzu-lu said, 'I should like to hear what you have set your heart on.'

The Master said, 'To bring peace to the old, to have trust in my friends, and to cherish the young.'

27. The Master said, 'I suppose I should give up hope. I have yet to meet the man who, on seeing his own errors, is able to take himself to task inwardly.'

28. The Master said, 'In a hamlet of ten households, there are bound to be those who are my equal in doing their best for others and in being trustworthy in what they say, but they are unlikely to be as eager to learn as I am.'

Book VI

1. The Master said, 'Yung could be given the seat facing south.'*

2. Chung-kung asked about Tzu-sang Po-tzu. The Master said, 'It is his simplicity of style that makes him acceptable.'

Chung-kung said, 'In ruling over the common people, is it not acceptable to hold oneself in reverence and merely to be simple in the measures one takes? On the other hand, is it not carrying simplicity too far to be simple in the way one holds oneself as well as in the measures one takes?'

The Master said, 'Yung is right in what he says.'

3. When Duke Ai asked which of his disciples was eager to learn, Confucius answered, 'There was one Yen Hui who was eager to learn. He did not vent his anger upon an innocent person, nor did he make the same mistake twice. Unfortunately his allotted span was a short one and he died. Now there is no one. No one eager to learn has come to my notice.'

4. Jan Tzu asked for grain for the mother of Tzu-hua who was away on a mission to Ch'i. The Master said,

---

* The seat of the ruler.

'Give her one *fu*.'* Jan Tzu asked for more. 'Give her one *yü*.' Jan Tzu gave her five *ping* of grain.

The Master said, 'Ch'ih went off to Ch'i drawn by well-fed horses and wearing light furs. I have heard it said, A gentleman gives to help the needy and not to maintain the rich in style.'

5. On becoming his† steward, Yüan Ssu was given nine hundred measures of grain which he declined. The Master said, 'Can you not find a use for it in helping the people in your neighbourhood?'

6. The Master said of Chung-kung, 'Should a bull born of plough cattle have a sorrel coat and well-formed horns, would the spirits of the mountains and rivers allow it to be passed over even if we felt it was not good enough to be used?'

7. The Master said, 'In his heart for three months at a time Hui does not lapse from benevolence. The others attain benevolence merely by fits and starts.'

8. Chi K'ang Tzu asked, 'Is Chung Yu good enough to be given office?'

The Master said, 'Yu is resolute. What difficulties could there be for him in taking office?'

'Is Ssu good enough to be given office?'

'Ssu is a man of understanding. What difficulties could there be for him in taking office?'

'Is Ch'iu good enough to be given office?'

---

* *Fu*, *yü* and *ping* are dry measures in ascending order of capacity.
† i.e., Confucius'.

'Ch'iu is accomplished. What difficulties could there be for him in taking office?'

9. The Chi Family wanted to make Min Tzu-ch'ien the steward of Pi. Min Tzu-ch'ien said, 'Decline the offer for me tactfully. If anyone comes back for me, I shall be on the other side of the River Wen.'*

10. Po-niu was ill. The Master visited him and, holding his hand through the window, said, 'We are going to lose him. It must be Destiny. Why else should such a man be stricken with such a disease? Why else should such a man be stricken with such a disease?'

11. The Master said, 'How admirable Hui is! Living in a mean dwelling on a bowlful of rice and a ladleful of water is a hardship most men would find intolerable, but Hui does not allow this to affect his joy. How admirable Hui is!'

12. Jan Ch'iu said, 'It is not that I am not pleased with your way, but rather that my strength gives out.' The Master said, 'A man whose strength gives out collapses along the course. In your case you set the limits beforehand.'

13. The Master said to Tzu-hsia, 'Be a gentleman *ju*,† not a petty *ju*.'

---

* i.e., over the border into the state of Ch'i.
† The original meaning of the word is uncertain, but it probably referred to men for whom the qualities of the scholar were more important than those of the warrior. In subsequent ages, *ju* came to be the name given to the Confucianists.

14. Tzu-yu was the steward of Wu Ch'eng. The Master said, 'Have you made any discoveries there?'

'There is one T'an-t'ai Mieh-ming who never takes short-cuts and who has never been to my room except on official business.'

15. The Master said, 'Meng chih Fan was not given to boasting. When the army was routed, he stayed in the rear. But on entering the gate, he goaded his horse on, saying, 'I did not lag behind out of presumption. It was simply that my horse refused to go forward.'

16. The Master said, 'You may have the good looks of Sung Chao, but you will find it difficult to escape unscathed in this world if you do not, at the same time, have the eloquence of the Priest T'uo.'

17. The Master said, 'Who can go out without using the door? Why, then, does no one follow this Way?'

18. The Master said, 'When there is a preponderance of native substance over acquired refinement, the result will be churlishness. When there is a preponderance of acquired refinement over native substance, the result will be pedantry. Only a well-balanced admixture of these two will result in gentlemanliness.'

19. The Master said, 'That a man lives is because he is straight. That a man who dupes others survives is because he has been fortunate enough to be spared.'

20. The Master said, 'To be fond of something is better than merely to know it, and to find joy in it is better than merely to be fond of it.'

21. The Master said, 'You can tell those who are above average about the best, but not those who are below average.'

22. Fan Ch'ih asked about wisdom. The Master said, 'To work for the things the common people have a right to and to keep one's distance from the gods and spirits while showing them reverence can be called wisdom.'

Fan Ch'ih asked about benevolence. The Master said, 'The benevolent man reaps the benefit only after overcoming difficulties. That can be called benevolence.'

23. The Master said, 'The wise find joy in water; the benevolent find joy in mountains. The wise are active; the benevolent are still. The wise are joyful; the benevolent are long-lived.'

24. The Master said, 'At one stroke Ch'i can be made into a Lu, and Lu, at one stroke, can be made to attain the Way.'

25. The Master said, 'A *ku** that is not truly a *ku*. A *ku* indeed! A *ku* indeed!'

26. Tsai Wo asked, 'If a benevolent man was told that there was another benevolent man in the well, would he, nevertheless, go and join him?'

The Master said, 'Why should that be the case? A gentleman can be sent there, but cannot be lured into a trap. He can be deceived, but cannot be duped.'

27. The Master said, 'The gentleman widely versed in

* A drinking vessel with a regulation capacity.

culture but brought back to essentials by the rites can, I suppose, be relied upon not to turn against what he stood for.'

28. The Master went to see Nan Tzu.* Tzu-lu was displeased. The Master swore, 'If I have done anything improper, may Heaven's curse be on me, may Heaven's curse be on me!'

29. The Master said, 'Supreme indeed is the Mean as a moral virtue. It has been rare among the common people for quite a long time.'

30. Tzu-kung said, 'If there were a man who gave extensively to the common people and brought help to the multitude, what would you think of him? Could he be called benevolent?'

The Master said, 'It is no longer a matter of benevolence with such a man. If you must describe him, "sage" is, perhaps, the right word. Even Yao and Shun would have found it difficult to accomplish as much. Now, on the other hand, a benevolent man helps others to take their stand in so far as he himself wishes to take his stand,† and gets others there in so far as he himself wishes to get there. The ability to take as analogy what is near at hand‡ can be called the method of benevolence.'

---

* The notorious wife of Duke Ling of Wei.
† It is on the rites that one takes one's stand. Cf. 'Take your stand on the rites' (VIII.8).
‡ viz., oneself.

Book VII

1. The Master said, 'I transmit but do not innovate; I am truthful in what I say and devoted to antiquity. I venture to compare myself to our Old P'eng.'*

2. The Master said, 'Quietly to store up knowledge in my mind, to learn without flagging, to teach without growing weary, these present me with no difficulties.'

3. The Master said, 'It is these things that cause me concern: failure to cultivate virtue, failure to go more deeply into what I have learned, inability, when I am told what is right, to move to where it is, and inability to reform myself when I have defects.'

4. During his leisure moments, the Master remained correct though relaxed.

5. The Master said, 'How I have gone downhill! It has been such a long time since I dreamt of the Duke of Chou.'

6. The Master said, 'I set my heart on the Way, base myself on virtue, lean upon benevolence for support and take my recreation in the arts.'

7. The Master said, 'I have never denied instruction to anyone who, of his own accord, has given me so much as a bundle of dried meat as a present.'

* It is not clear who Old P'eng was.

8. The Master said, 'I never enlighten anyone who has not been driven to distraction by trying to understand a difficulty or who has not got into a frenzy trying to put his ideas into words.

'When I have pointed out one corner of a square to anyone and he does not come back with the other three, I will not point it out to him a second time.'

9. When eating in the presence of one who had been bereaved, the Master never ate his fill.

10. On a day he had wept, the Master did not sing.

11. The Master said to Yen Yüan, 'Only you and I have the ability to go forward when employed and to stay out of sight when set aside.'

Tzu-lu said, 'If you were leading the Three Armies whom would you take with you?'

The Master said, 'I would not take with me anyone who would try to fight a tiger with his bare hands or to walk across the River* and die in the process without regrets. If I took anyone it would have to be a man who, when faced with a task, was fearful of failure and who, while fond of making plans, was capable of successful execution.'

12. The Master said, 'If wealth were a permissible pursuit, I would be willing even to act as a guard holding a whip outside the market place. If it is not, I shall follow my own preferences.'

---

* In ancient Chinese literature, 'the River' meant the Yellow River.

13. Fasting, war and sickness were the things over which the Master exercised care.

14. The Master heard the *shao** in Ch'i and for three months did not notice the taste of the meat he ate. He said, 'I never dreamt that the joys of music could reach such heights.'

15. Jan Yu said, 'Is the Master on the side of the Lord of Wei?'† Tzu-kung said, 'Well, I shall put the question to him.'

He went in and said, 'What sort of men were Po Yi and Shu Ch'i?'

'They were excellent men of old.'

'Did they have any complaints?'

'They sought benevolence and got it. So why should they have any complaints?'

When Tzu-kung came out, he said, 'The Master is not on his side.'

16. The Master said, 'In the eating of coarse rice and the drinking of water, the using of one's elbow for a pillow, joy is to be found. Wealth and rank attained through

---

* The music of Shun. Cf. III.25.

† i.e., Che, known in history as the Ousted Duke, son of Prince K'uai K'ui who was son of Duke Ling. After failing in an attempt to kill Nan Tzu, the notorious wife of his father, Prince K'uai K'ui fled to Chin. On the death of Duke Ling, Che came to the throne. With the backing of the Chin army, Prince K'uai K'ui managed to install himself in the city of Ch'i in Wei, waiting for an opportunity to oust his son. At that time Confucius was in Wei, and what Jan Yu wanted to know was whether he was for Che.

immoral means have as much to do with me as passing clouds.'

17. The Master said, 'Grant me a few more years so that I may study at the age of fifty and I shall be free from major errors.'

18. What the Master used the correct pronunciation for: the *Odes*, the *Book of History* and the performance of the rites. In all these cases he used the correct pronunciation.

19. The Governor of She asked Tzu-lu about Confucius. Tzu-lu did not answer. The Master said, 'Why did you not simply say something to this effect: he is the sort of man who forgets to eat when he tries to solve a problem that has been driving him to distraction, who is so full of joy that he forgets his worries and who does not notice the onset of old age?'

20. The Master said, 'I was not born with knowledge but, being fond of antiquity, I am quick to seek it.'

21. The topics the Master did not speak of were prodigies, force, disorder and gods.

22. The Master said, 'Even when walking in the company of two other men, I am bound to be able to learn from them. The good points of the one I copy; the bad points of the other I correct in myself.'

23. The Master said, 'Heaven is author of the virtue that is in me. What can Huan T'ui do to me?'*

---

* According to tradition, this was said on the occasion when Huan T'ui, the Minister of War in Sung, attempted to kill him.

24. The Master said, 'My friends, do you think I am secretive? There is nothing which I hide from you. There is nothing I do which I do not share with you, my friends. There is Ch'iu for you.'

25. The Master instructs under four heads: culture, moral conduct, doing one's best and being trustworthy in what one says.

26. The Master said, 'I have no hopes of meeting a sage. I would be content if I met someone who is a gentleman.'

The Master said, 'I have no hopes of meeting a good man. I would be content if I met someone who has constancy. It is hard for a man to have constancy who claims to have when he is wanting, to be full when he is empty and to be comfortable when he is in straitened circumstances.'

27. The Master used a fishing line but not a cable;* he used a corded arrow but not to shoot at roosting birds.

28. The Master said, 'There are presumably men who innovate without possessing knowledge, but that is not a fault I have. I use my ears widely and follow what is good in what I have heard; I use my eyes widely and retain what I have seen in my mind. This constitutes a lower level of knowledge.'

29. People of Hu Hsiang were difficult to talk to. A boy was received and the disciples were perplexed. The Master said, 'Approval of his coming does not mean approval of him when he is not here. Why should we be

---

* Attached to a net.

so exacting? When a man comes after having purified himself, we approve of his purification but we cannot vouch for his past.'*

30. The Master said, 'Is benevolence really far away? No sooner do I desire it than it is here.'

31. Ch'en Ssu-pai asked whether Duke Chao was versed in the rites. Confucius said, 'Yes.'

After Confucius had gone, Ch'en Ssu-pai, bowing to Wu-ma Ch'i, invited him forward and said, 'I have heard that the gentleman does not show partiality. Does he show it nevertheless? The Lord took as wife a daughter of Wu, who thus is of the same clan as himself,† but he allows her to be called Wu Meng Tzu.‡ If the Lord is versed in the rites, who isn't?'

When Wu-ma Ch'i recounted this to him, the Master said, 'I am a fortunate man. Whenever I make a mistake, other people are sure to notice it.'§

32. When the Master was singing in the company of others and liked someone else's song, he always asked to hear it again before joining in.

33. The Master said, 'In unstinted effort I can compare

---

* It has been suggested that this sentence should stand at the beginning of Confucius' remark.
† Bearing the name Chi.
‡ when she should be called Wu Chi. Calling her Wu Meng Tzu was an attempt to gloss over the fact that she shared the same clan name of Chi.
§ Being a native of Lu, Confucius would rather be criticized for partiality than appear to be openly critical of the Duke.

with others, but in being a practising gentleman I have had, as yet, no success.'

34. The Master said, 'How dare I claim to be a sage or a benevolent man? Perhaps it might be said of me that I learn without flagging and teach without growing weary.' Kung-hsi Hua said, 'This is precisely where we disciples are unable to learn from your example.'

35. The Master was seriously ill. Tzu-lu asked permission to offer a prayer. The Master said, 'Was such a thing ever done?' Tzu-lu said, 'Yes, it was. The prayer offered was as follows: pray thus to the gods above and below.' The Master said, 'In that case, I have long been offering my prayers.'

36. The Master said, 'Extravagance means ostentation, frugality means shabbiness. I would rather be shabby than ostentatious.'

37. The Master said, 'The gentleman is easy of mind, while the small man is always full of anxiety.'

38. The Master is cordial yet stern, awe-inspiring yet not fierce, and respectful yet at ease.

Book VIII

1. The Master said, 'Surely T'ai Po can be said to be of the highest virtue. Three times he abdicated his right to rule over the Empire, and yet he left behind nothing the common people could acclaim.'

2. The Master said, 'Unless a man has the spirit of the rites, in being respectful he will wear himself out, in being careful he will become timid, in having courage he will become unruly, and in being forthright he will become intolerant.

'When the gentleman feels profound affection for his parents, the common people will be stirred to benevolence. When he does not forget friends of long standing, the common people will not shirk their obligations to other people.'

3. When he was seriously ill Tseng Tzu summoned his disciples and said, 'Take a look at my hands. Take a look at my feet. The *Odes* say,

> In fear and trembling,
> As if approaching a deep abyss,
> As if walking on thin ice.*

* Ode 195.

Only now am I sure of being spared,* my young friends.'

4. Tseng Tzu was seriously ill. When Meng Ching Tzu visited him, this was what Tseng Tzu said,

> 'Sad is the cry of a dying bird;
> Good are the words of a dying man.

There are three things which the gentleman values most in the Way: to stay clear of violence by putting on a serious countenance, to come close to being trusted by setting a proper expression on his face, and to avoid being boorish and unreasonable by speaking in proper tones. As for the business of sacrificial vessels, there are officials responsible for that.'

5. Tseng Tzu said, 'To be able yet to ask the advice of those who are not able. To have many talents yet to ask the advice of those who have few. To have yet to appear to want. To be full yet to appear empty.† To be transgressed against yet not to mind. It was towards this end that my friend‡ used to direct his efforts.'

6. Tseng Tzu said, 'If a man can be entrusted with an orphan six *ch'ih*§ tall, and the fate of a state one hundred *li* square, without his being deflected from his purpose

* i.e., to have avoided, now that he was on the point of death, the risk of the mutilation of his body – a duty which he owed to his parents.

† This is in contrast to the man 'who claims to have when he is wanting, to be full when he is empty' (VII.26).

‡ According to tradition, this refers to Yen Hui.

§ The *ch'ih* in Tseng Tzu's time was much shorter than the modern foot.

even in moments of crisis, is he not a gentleman? He is, indeed, a gentleman.'

7. Tseng Tzu said, 'A Gentleman must be strong and resolute, for his burden is heavy and the road is long. He takes benevolence as his burden. Is that not heavy? Only with death does the road come to an end. Is that not long?'

8. The Master said, 'Be stimulated by the *Odes*, take your stand on the rites and be perfected by music.'

9. The Master said, 'The common people can be made to follow a path but not to understand it.'

10. The Master said, 'Being fond of courage while detesting poverty will lead men to unruly behaviour. Excessive detestation of men who are not benevolent will provoke them to unruly behaviour.'

11. The Master said, 'Even with a man as gifted as the Duke of Chou, if he was arrogant and miserly, then the rest of his qualities would not be worthy of admiration.'

12. The Master said, 'It is not easy to find a man who can study for three years without thinking about earning a salary.'

13. The Master said, 'Have the firm faith to devote yourself to learning, and abide to the death in the good way. Enter not a state that is in peril; stay not in a state that is in danger. Show yourself when the Way prevails in the Empire, but hide yourself when it does not. It is a shameful matter to be poor and humble when the Way

prevails in the state. Equally, it is a shameful matter to be rich and noble when the Way falls into disuse in the state.'

14. The Master said, 'Do not concern yourself with matters of government unless they are the responsibility of your office.'

15. The Master said, 'When Chih, the Master Musician, begins to play and when the *Kuan chü** comes to its end, how the sound fills the ear!'

16. The Master said, 'Men who reject discipline and yet are not straight, men who are ignorant and yet not cautious, men who are devoid of ability and yet not trustworthy are quite beyond my understanding.'

17. The Master said, 'Even with a man who urges himself on in his studies as though he was losing ground, my fear is still that he may not make it in time.'

18. The Master said, 'How lofty Shun and Yü were in holding aloof from the Empire when they were in possession of it.'

19. The Master said, 'Great indeed was Yao as a ruler! How lofty! It is Heaven that is great and it was Yao who modelled himself upon it. He was so boundless that the common people were not able to put a name to his virtues. Lofty was he in his successes and brilliant was he in his accomplishments!'

* The first ode in the *Odes*.

20. Shun had five officials and the Empire was well governed. King Wu said, 'I have ten capable officials.'

Confucius commented, 'How true it is that talent is difficult to find! The period of T'ang and Yü* was rich in talent.† With a woman amongst them, there were, in fact, only nine.‡ The Chou continued to serve the Yin when it was in possession of two-thirds of the Empire. Its virtue can be said to have been the highest.'

21. The Master said, 'With Yü I can find no fault. He ate and drank the meanest fare while making offerings to ancestral spirits and gods with the utmost devotion proper to a descendant. He wore coarse clothes while sparing no splendour in his robes and caps on sacrificial occasions. He lived in lowly dwellings while devoting all his energy to the building of irrigation canals. With Yü I can find no fault.'

* T'ang here is the name of Yao's dynasty and Yü the name of Shun's dynasty, not to be confused with T'ang the founder of the Yin or Shang dynasty and Yü the founder of the Hsia dynasty.
† Yet Shun had only five officials.
‡ In the case of King Wu.

Book IX

1. The occasions on which the Master talked about profit, Destiny and benevolence were rare.

2. A man from a village in Ta Hsiang said, 'Great indeed is Confucius! He has wide learning but has not made a name for himself in any field.' The Master, on hearing of this, said, to his disciples, 'What should I make myself proficient in? In driving? or in archery? I think I would prefer driving.'

3. The Master said, 'A ceremonial cap of linen is what is prescribed by the rites. Today black silk is used instead. This is more frugal and I follow the majority. To prostrate oneself before ascending the steps is what is prescribed by the rites. Today one does so after having ascended them. This is casual and, though going against the majority, I follow the practice of doing so before ascending.'

4. There were four things the Master refused to have anything to do with: he refused to entertain conjectures or insist on certainty; he refused to be inflexible or to be egotistical.

5. When under siege in K'uang, the Master said, 'With King Wen dead, is not culture (*wen*) invested here in me? If Heaven intends culture to be destroyed, those who

come after me will not be able to have any part of it. If Heaven does not intend this culture to be destroyed, then what can the men of K'uang do to me?'

6. The *t'ai tsai** asked Tzu-kung, 'Surely the Master is a sage, is he not? Otherwise why should he be skilled in so many things?' Tzu-kung said, 'It is true, Heaven set him on the path to sagehood. However, he is skilled in many things besides.'

The Master, on hearing of this, said, 'How well the *t'ai tsai* knows me! I was of humble station when young. That is why I am skilled in many menial things. Should a gentleman be skilled in many things? No, not at all.'

7. Lao† said, 'The Master said, "I have never been proved in office. That is why I am a Jack of all trades."'

8. The Master said, 'Do I possess knowledge? No, I do not. A rustic put a question to me and my mind was a complete blank. I kept hammering at the two sides of the question until I got everything out of it.'‡

9. The Master said, 'The Phoenix does not appear nor does the River offer up its Chart.§ I am done for.'

10. When the Master encountered men who were in

---

* This is the title of a high office. It is not clear who the person referred to was or even from which state he came.
† The identity of the person referred to here is uncertain.
‡ The whole section is exceedingly obscure and the translation is tentative.
§ Both the Phoenix and the Chart were auspicious omens. Confucius is here lamenting the hopelessness of putting the Way into practice in the Empire of his day.

mourning or in ceremonial cap and robes or were blind, he would, on seeing them, rise to his feet, even though they were younger than he was, and, on passing them, would quicken his step.*

11. Yen Yüan, heaving a sigh, said, 'The more I look up at it the higher it appears. The more I bore into it the harder it becomes. I see it before me. Suddenly it is behind me.

'The Master is good at leading one on step by step. He broadens me with culture and brings me back to essentials by means of the rites. I cannot give up even if I wanted to, but, having done all I can, it† seems to rise sheer above me and I have no way of going after it, however much I may want to.'

12. The Master was seriously ill. Tzu-lu told his disciples to act as retainers.‡ During a period when his condition had improved, the Master said, 'Yu has long been practising deception. In pretending that I had retainers when I had none, who would we be deceiving? Would we be deceiving Heaven? Moreover, would I not rather die in your hands, my friends, than in the hands of retainers? And even if I were not given an elaborate funeral, it is not as if I was dying by the wayside.'

13. Tzu-kung said, 'If you had a piece of beautiful jade here, would you put it away safely in a box or would

* as a sign of respect.
† Throughout this chapter the 'it' refers to the way of Confucius.
‡ When Confucius, no longer in office, was not in a position to have them.

you try to sell it for a good price?' The Master said, 'Of course I would sell it. Of course I would sell it. All I am waiting for is the right offer.'

14. The Master wanted to settle amongst the Nine Barbarian Tribes of the east. Someone said, 'But could you put up with their uncouth ways?' The Master said, 'Once a gentleman settles amongst them, what uncouthness will there be?'

15. The Master said, 'It was after my return from Wei to Lu that the music was put right, with the *ya* and the *sung** being assigned their proper places.'

16. The Master said, 'To serve high officials when abroad, and my elders when at home, in arranging funerals not to dare to spare myself, and to be able to hold my drink – these are trifles that give me no trouble.'

17. While standing by a river, the Master said, 'What passes away is, perhaps, like this. Day and night it never lets up.'

18. The Master said, 'I have yet to meet the man who is as fond of virtue as he is of beauty in women.'

19. The Master said, 'As in the case of making a mound, if, before the very last basketful, I stop, then I shall have stopped. As in the case of levelling the ground, if, though tipping only one basketful, I am going forward, then I shall be making progress.'

---

* The *ya* and the *sung* are sections in the *Odes*.

20. The Master said, 'If anyone can listen to me with unflagging attention, it is Hui, I suppose.'

21. The Master said of Yen Yüan, 'I watched him making progress, but I did not see him realize his capacity to the full. What a pity!'

22. The Master said, 'There are, are there not, young plants that fail to produce blossoms, and blossoms that fail to produce fruit?'

23. The Master said, 'It is fitting that we should hold the young in awe. How do we know that the generations to come will not be the equal of the present? Only when a man reaches the age of forty or fifty without distinguishing himself in any way can one say, I suppose, that he does not deserve to be held in awe.'

24. The Master said, 'One cannot but give assent to exemplary words, but what is important is that one should rectify oneself. One cannot but be pleased with tactful words, but what is important is that one should reform oneself. I can do nothing with the man who gives assent but does not rectify himself or the man who is pleased but does not reform himself.'

25. The Master said, 'Make it your guiding principle to do your best for others and to be trustworthy in what you say. Do not accept as friend anyone who is not as good as you. When you make a mistake do not be afraid of mending your ways.'

26. The Master said, 'The Three Armies can be deprived

of their commanding officer, but even a common man cannot be deprived of his purpose.'

27. The Master said, 'If anyone can, while dressed in a worn-out gown padded with old silk floss, stand beside a man wearing fox or badger fur without feeling ashamed, it is, I suppose, Yu.

> Neither envious nor covetous,
> How can he be anything but good?'*

Thereafter, Tzu-lu constantly recited these verses. The Master commented, 'The way summed up in these verses will hardly enable one to be good.'

28. The Master said, 'Only when the cold season comes is the point brought home that the pine and the cypress are the last to lose their leaves.'

29. The Master said, 'The man of wisdom is never in two minds;† the man of benevolence never worries;‡ the man of courage is never afraid.'

30. The Master said, 'A man good enough as a partner in one's studies need not be good enough as a partner in the pursuit of the Way; a man good enough as a partner in the pursuit of the Way need not be good enough as a partner in a common stand; a man good enough as a partner in a common stand need not be good enough as a partner in the exercise of moral discretion.'

---

* Ode 33.   † About right and wrong.   ‡ About the future.

31.

> The flowers of the cherry tree,
> How they wave about!
> It's not that I do not think of you,
> But your home is so far away.*

The Master commented, 'He did not really think of her. If he did, there is no such thing as being far away.'

* These lines are not to be found in the present *Odes*.

Book X

1. In the local community, Confucius was submissive and seemed to be inarticulate. In the ancestral temple and at court, though fluent, he did not speak lightly.

2. At court, when speaking with Counsellors of lower rank he was affable; when speaking with Counsellors of upper rank, he was frank though respectful. In the presence of his lord, his bearing, though respectful, was composed.

3. When he was summoned by his lord to act as usher, his face took on a serious expression and his step became brisk. When he bowed to his colleagues, stretching out his hands to the left or to the right, his robes followed his movements without being disarranged. He went forward with quickened steps, as though he was gliding on wings. After the withdrawal of the guest, he invariably reported, 'The guest has stopped looking back.'

4. On going through the outer gates to his lord's court, he drew himself in, as though the entrance was too small to admit him.

When he stood, he did not occupy the centre of the gateway;* when he walked, he did not step on the threshold.

* A position which would have been presumptuous.

When he went past the station of his lord, his face took on a serious expression, his step became brisk, and his words seemed more laconic.

When he lifted the hem of his robe to ascend the hall, he drew himself in, stopped inhaling as if he had no need to breathe.

When he had come out and descended the first step, relaxing his expression, he seemed no longer to be tense.

When he had reached the bottom of the steps he went forward with quickened steps as though he was gliding on wings.

When he resumed his station, his bearing was respectful.

5. When he held the jade tablet, he drew himself in as though its weight was too much for him. He held the upper part of the tablet as though he was bowing; he held the lower part of the tablet as though he was ready to hand over a gift. His expression was solemn as though in fear and trembling, and his feet were constrained as though following a marked line.

When making a presentation, his expression was genial.

At a private audience, he was relaxed.

6. The gentleman avoided using dark purple and maroon coloured silk for lapels and cuffs. Red and violet coloured silks were not used for informal dress.

When, in the heat of summer, he wore an unlined robe made of either fine or coarse material, he invariably wore it over an underrobe to set it off.

Under a black jacket, he wore lambskin; under an undyed jacket, he wore fawnskin; under a yellow jacket, he wore fox fur.

His informal fur coat was long but with a short right sleeve.

He invariably had a night robe which was half as long again as he was tall.*

Their fur being thick, pelts of the fox and the badger were used as rugs.

Once the period of mourning was over, he placed no restrictions on the kind of ornament that he wore.

Other than skirts for ceremonial occasions, everything else was made up from cut pieces.

Lambskin coats and black caps were not used on visits of condolence.

On New Year's Day, he invariably went to court in court dress.

7. In periods of purification, he invariably wore a house robe made of the cheaper sort of material.

In periods of purification, he invariably changed to a more austere diet and, when at home, did not sit in his usual place.

8. He did not eat his fill of polished rice, nor did he eat his fill of finely minced meat.

He did not eat rice that had gone sour or fish and meat that had spoiled. He did not eat food that had gone off colour or food that had a bad smell. He did not

---

*It has been suggested that this sentence has got out of place and should follow the first sentence in the next section.

eat food that was not properly prepared nor did he eat except at the proper times. He did not eat food that had not been properly cut up, nor did he eat unless the proper sauce was available.

Even when there was plenty of meat, he avoided eating more meat than rice.

Only in the case of wine did he not set himself a rigid limit. He simply never drank to the point of becoming confused.

He did not consume wine or dried meat bought from a shop.

Even when he did not have the side dish of ginger cleared from the table, he did not eat more than was proper.

9. After assisting at a sacrifice at his lord's place, he did not keep his portion of the sacrificial meat overnight. In other cases, he did not keep the sacrificial meat for more than three days. Once it was kept beyond three days he no longer ate it.

10. He did not converse at meals; nor did he talk in bed.

11. Even when a meal consisted only of coarse rice and vegetable broth, he invariably made an offering from them and invariably did so solemnly.

12. He did not sit, unless his mat was straight.

13. When drinking at a village gathering, he left as soon as those carrying walking sticks had left.

14. When the villagers were exorcizing evil spirits, he stood in his court robes on the eastern steps.*

15. When making inquiries after someone in another state, he bowed to the ground twice before sending off the messenger.

16. When K'ang Tzu sent a gift of medicine, [Confucius] bowed his head to the ground before accepting it. However, he said, 'Not knowing its properties, I dare not taste it.'

17. The stables caught fire. The Master, on returning from court, asked, 'Was anyone hurt?' He did not ask about the horses.

18. When his lord gave a gift of cooked food, the first thing he invariably did was to taste it after having adjusted his mat. When his lord gave him a gift of uncooked food, he invariably cooked it and offered it to the ancestors. When his lord gave him a gift of a live animal, he invariably reared it. At the table of his lord, when his lord had made an offering before the meal he invariably started with the rice first.

19. During an illness, when his lord paid him a visit, he would lie with his head to the east, with his court robes draped over him and his grand sash trailing over the side of the bed.

20. When summoned by his lord, he would set off without waiting for horses to be yoked to his carriage.

* The place for a host to stand.

21. When he went inside the Grand Temple, he asked questions about everything.

22. Whenever a friend died who had no kin to whom his body could be taken, he said, 'Let him be given a funeral from my house.'

23. Even when a gift from a friend was a carriage and horses – since it lacked the solemnity of sacrificial meat – he did not bow to the ground.

24. When in bed, he did not lie like a corpse, nor did he sit in the formal manner of a guest when by himself.

25. When he met a bereaved person in mourning dress, even though it was someone he was on familiar terms with, he invariably assumed a solemn expression. When he met someone wearing a ceremonial cap or someone blind, even though they were well-known to him, he invariably showed them respect.

On passing a person dressed as a mourner he would lean forward with his hands on the cross-bar of his carriage to show respect; he would act in a similar manner towards a person carrying official documents.

When a sumptuous feast was brought on, he invariably assumed a solemn expression and rose to his feet.

When there was a sudden clap of thunder or a violent wind, he invariably assumed a solemn attitude.

26. When climbing into a carriage, he invariably stood squarely and grasped the mounting-cord.

When in the carriage, he did not turn towards the inside, nor did he shout or point.

27. Startled, the bird rose up and circled round before alighting. He said, 'The female pheasant on the mountain bridge, how timely her action is, how timely her action is!' Tzu-lu cupped one hand in the other in a gesture of respect towards the bird which, flapping its wings three times, flew away.